D0966074

TWIN KILLING

MARSHALL COOK

TWIN KILLING

MARSHALL COOK

BLEAK HOUSE BOOKS

MADISON | WISCONSIN

Published by Bleak House Books
a division of Big Earth Publishing
923 Williamson St.
Madison, WI 53703
www.bleakhousebooks.com

This is a work of fiction. Any similarities to people or places, living or dead, is purely coincidental.

ISBN 13 (cloth): 978-1-932557-38-1

Library of Congress Cataloging-in-Publication Data has been applied for.

Printed in the United States of America

11 10 09 08 07   1 2 3 4 5 6 7 8 9 10

To Marion Mitchell Morrison

Monona Quinn accelerates into the curve, her little del Sol skittering slightly before regaining traction.

She is late. Very late. And Doug will be very angry.

Resentment surges through her. Let him be angry! The thought shames her.

She promised to be home by 6:00, and now it's after 8:00. But this time it isn't her fault, it really isn't.

Keeping her eyes on the road, she fumbles the cell phone out of her purse and speed dials their home number. Might as well break another Doug Stennett rule, the one about using the cell while driving.

Pick up, she thinks. Pick up!

But he doesn't pick up, a very bad sign.

In the beginning, she'd worked late several times a week, putting in 80-90-even 100-hour weeks, on-the-job training in editing what she soon came to think of as "the weekly miracle." Doug had been patient then. Sometimes he barely seemed to notice, in fact, so hard was he working to establish himself as a financial analyst. But as his consulting business began to thrive, his patience evaporated, leaving sarcasm and a hangdog martyrdom that infuriated her.

Tonight she had intended to get home on time, no matter what; tonight was to be a celebration of their first two years in Mitchell—candlelight dinner and a rented DVD, *Murphy's Romance*, which they'd wanted to see together for ages.

She tries to urge a little more speed out of the car without sliding off onto the loose gravel of the shoulder. In rural Wisconsin, roads bend to accommodate the farms, and she has to skirt the sprawling Huibregtse acreage before reaching home.

Rounding the last curve, she at last sees their one-story farmhouse perched on the hill, shaded by a huge maple tree. She downshifts as she swings into the long, winding driveway. She had planned to shower and put on the blue silk jammies Doug referred to as "foxy"—and here she is, still in jeans and flannel shirt, redolent of grease and onions from the burger Bruce fetched from the diner for her lunch.

She swings in beside Doug's CR-V, cuts the engine, and vaults out of the car, leaving her briefcase and exchange newspapers on the passenger seat. Maybe it won't be so bad, she thinks, as she pounds up the wooden steps and onto the deck that wraps around three sides of the house.

It's worse.

She bursts through the front door and hurries through the living room to the kitchen, where some sort of elaborate chicken dish, long past cooling, sits on a platter under a cake cover on the counter.

"Doug? Hello?"

She hustles back through the living room, confronting the closed door of his office.

"Doug?"

As she reaches for the doorknob, the door opens, and Doug stands in the doorway. He's wearing his navy blue suit pants, a crisp, white dress shirt, and a blue-and-yellow-striped tie. His long, lean runner's body looks so good in that suit, and his clean, sharp features and wavy, black hair render him handsome despite the slightly nerdy, wire-rim glasses that perpetually slide down his nose and the sheepish half grin he so often wears.

He doesn't look sheepish now; he looks like the dinner sitting on the counter in the kitchen, elegant but cold.

"Oh, Doug. I'm so sorry! I really couldn't help it! Pierpont installed new pagination software, and it was just a mess."

His stony face reveals no emotion. His "Mount Rushmore," she calls it.

He's worse than angry. He's hurt. A pang of guilt strikes her, and then an electric jolt of resentment, which she fights down.

"Is dinner ruined? We could go out. I know! Let's watch the movie and eat popcorn and ice cream!"

Her words break against his stony countenance.

"I couldn't help it, Doug. Pierpont installed the new system overnight and insisted that we use it today—publication day! I thought Bruce was going to strangle him."

Getting no response, she plunges on.

"The write-up of the Common Council meeting got wiped off the hard drive, columns kept sliding off the page, whole pages disappeared into cyberspace. By the time we finally got the whole mess nailed down, it was 7:30.

"With the new system, we're supposed to be able to transmit the layouts to the printer electronically, but even Bruce couldn't figure out how to do that. He volunteered to drive everything over to the printers for me, God bless him."

"God bless Bruce. What would we do without good old Bruce?"

She swallows hard, determined not to get drawn into a

shouting match. At least he finally said something. "Were you working?" She nods toward the computer screen behind him. The screen casts a pale blue aura in the otherwise dark room.

"Nope. Article for SABR. A statistical analysis of the importance of WHIP and earned run average to a pitcher's overall worth to his team. Something to wile away the hours while waiting for my wife."

"You didn't expect me to just dump everything on Vi and Bruce, did you?"

"No, no. I wouldn't want you to do something like that to Vi and Bruce."

"I'm the editor, Doug. The *Doings* is my responsibility."

"Right. Absolutely. I understand. I'm only the husband here."

"What do you want from me, Douglas? Do you want me to quit? I did that once, remember? I gave up a job most writers would kill for to—"

The phone rings in the kitchen.

"Better answer that," Doug says, his eyes looking past her. "There's probably some problem with the paper."

Her anger spikes, and she is about to snap back when foreboding floods her. "It's Maddie," she says, frowning. "Something's wrong."

She turns and retreats to the kitchen, catching the phone on the fifth ring, just before the answering machine would have picked up.

"Hello?"

"Thank God you're there!" Mo was right, it is Maddie.

"What's wrong? Is Mom . . .?"

"Mom's fine. It's Aidan."

The picture that springs to mind is sadly out of date—a

sweet, happy boy running to greet her and hug her leg. He called her his "Mommy two"—or maybe he was saying "Mommy, too." The picture dissolves with Maddie's next words.

"He's been arrested."

"Arrested for what?"

"Possession of marijuana."

"Aidan?"

Doug's dress shoes click on the hardwood floor of the living room; he stands behind her in the kitchen doorway. A large metal bowl, still three-quarters full of unclaimed Halloween candy, sits on the kitchen counter next to the phone. Mo had been so disappointed when only a few kids came to their door for trick-or-treat. Even the sullen teenagers who came late, thrusting their bags out as if they were robbing a convenience store, had been better than the long stretches of silence that underscored their isolation.

"I didn't know who else to call," Maddie is saying. "What's going to happen, Sis?"

Mo takes a deep breath, willing herself to be calm in the face of her twin's near hysteria. "Have you got a lawyer?"

"Dan."

"I don't think Dan does criminal law."

She hears the quick intake of breath. Maddie is still processing her new, horrible reality, a bit at a time. Mo snatches a Reeses candy bar from the bowl and unwraps it, cradling the phone to her ear with her shoulder.

"The sheriff said something about a public defender," Maddie says.

"No. No public defender." Mo jams the candy into her mouth. She turns, twisting the phone cord around her finger, and her eyes meet Doug's. He mouths the single word, Who?

"Aidan," she whispers, and then, into the phone, she says, "Is Lewis Crubb still practicing law in town?"

"Lewis? I think so. I haven't seen him in ages."

Mo grabs another piece of candy. "Have you told Kenny?"

"Not yet."

"But you've heard from him recently, right?"

"Three days ago. He says he's fine and not to worry. You know Kenny."

Something clicks shut in Mo's mind, a decision made before she has been consciously aware of weighing it. "I'm coming," she says.

"Oh, Sis. I couldn't ask you to do that."

"You didn't ask. I'm volunteering."

"Maybe you could talk to him. He might listen to you."

She hears the tentative note of hope in her sister's voice and aches to do everything she can to keep it there. But what about the paper?

Mo had taken over the Prairie Rapids *Reporter* for three weeks in September while Sy Davidson was on vacation. He could return the favor now. Vi and Bruce could certainly handle the day-to-day without her.

And what about Doug?

"My mind's made up, kiddo," she says into the phone. "I'll get things squared away here and hop in the car, probably late tomorrow morning. I should be there for supper."

"Thank you so much. You don't know what this means to me."

"You just hang in. The cavalry's on its way."

She hangs up, her back still to Doug, and wrestles with the candy, which obstinately refuses to shed its wrapper. Giving up, she tosses it back into the bowl. "We should throw this junk out," she says.

Finally, she turns and meets his eyes. There is no anger in them now, only that maddening look of hurt and bewilderment and betrayal.

"Just like that."

"Doug, she needs me. Who else does she have?"

Doug takes a deep breath, as if preparing himself for the blindfold and cigarette.

"I owe it to her, Doug. I'm the one who ran off while she stayed on the farm. She's taken care of Mom all these years."

He stands only two strides from her, but as she searches for some sign of understanding in his eyes, he seems to stare back from across a vast abyss.

Absently, he loosens his tie and pulls the knot down. When he tries to unbutton his collar, the button pops off and pings on the floor.

"I can't promise I'll be here when you get back."

The words feel like a slap. "You can't mean that."

He runs his hands through his silky, black hair and then rams them in his pockets and hunches his shoulders. He takes another deep breath, blows it out through his nostrils, and with his forefinger pushes his glasses back up onto the bridge of his nose. "I don't know what I mean right now. You do what you need to do."

"Douglas, I . . ."

She takes a step toward him, and he puts a hand up, his eyes clouded with feeling.

"You go ahead. I'll be fine." His voice is controlled, quiet.

His shoes click on the hardwood floor as he crosses the living room. His office door shuts quietly behind him.

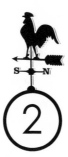

For over 250 miles, suspended between two worlds, Mo hasn't felt sure whether she is leaving or returning home. Now, as she nears the town where she grew up, the landscape becomes eerily familiar. She follows a turn in the road, spots a train trestle crossing the road 20 yards ahead, and realizes that she knew it would be there; knew, too, that graffiti would be spray-painted on the concrete beneath the steel railing.

She has many vivid mental images of her growing-up place. Now those images will be tested against home as it really is.

The road dips as she crosses underneath the trestle. She once stood on that trestle, holding hands with the boy she intended to spend the rest of her life with, looking down the tracks toward their future.

A song runs through her mind, *their* song, "When Doves Cry," by Prince. It evokes a yearning she hadn't thought herself still capable of.

Get a grip, girl, she warns herself.

She turns on the radio and scans to 1700 AM, KBGG Des Moines, and gets the afternoon farm report. She hits Seek, and the numbers wrap to the bottom of the dial, stopping at

640 AM, National Public Radio out of Iowa State in Ames; the familiar voices of Robert Siegel and Michele Norris soothe her.

Perhaps it's the unmistakable smell of pig that makes her memories so vivid.

Folks who complain about cows or horses should live near a pig farm, she thinks.

Another turn reveals a familiar barn and farmhouse, and she could swear the same cows are lying in the shade on a small rise to the left of the barn as were there the last time she drove by.

Life here has simply gone on without her, while her memories have remained frozen. She wonders how much will have changed.

A brown four-door sedan with "Sheriff of Falkner County" on the driver's side door and a red light on the roof pulls off the shoulder of the road and slides in behind her. This stretch of highway is a notorious speed trap, with a lone 55 mph speed limit sign posted just off the interstate and then not another reminder for the 14-mile stretch to town. Mo sets cruise control to 54, and they crawl along the gently curving road together, the sheriff's car staying a consistent distance behind her.

She unwraps a candy bar and chews it slowly, the chocolate making her choke until her eyes water. She threw away most of the Halloween candy before she left, sticking a last handful in her jacket pocket. If she hadn't tossed it, the candy would still be right where she left it when she got back. Doug could pass a candy bowl dozens of times a day without taking a single piece.

Will Doug still be there when you get back?

Just drive, she tells herself.

The county mountie is still behind her, with another car behind him.

A sneeze surprises her, then another, and then a third. It should be too late in the season for allergies, but obviously something in the air is attacking her.

As she approaches a crossroad, the sheriff's car signals a right turn. As she watches in the rearview mirror, he pulls off, letting the car behind him pass, and then pulls back in behind the second car. This guy is really out to get her!

But he's missed his chance. Her heartbeat quickens as she rounds the last curve and the little county highway turns into Main Street, Summerfeld, Iowa.

She clicks off the radio, slowing to the prescribed 25 mph, and focuses on the noble two-story homes set far back from the road in well-tended yards, full porches inviting neighbors to sit and visit. Splashes of red and yellow still cling defiantly to the trees. Mounds of fallen leaves wait in neat piles on parkways.

She is at the eastern end of the cruisers' loop. She wonders if high school kids still observe the Friday night ritual of piling into their cars and driving around Courthouse Square, up Church Road to Water Street, right on Water, right on Hammond, right on Main, and back around the square.

She remembers the sense of belonging she felt then, nestled in her boyfriend's arm, their music on the car radio, going nowhere on a Friday night.

Get a grip! Senior Prom's over!

As she reaches the square, her heart again surges. She passes Wallace's Pharmacy, a realty office, and then, on the corner, The Cowboy Craig Marvel Museum. It looks exactly as she remembers, with the plastic replica of Cowboy Craig himself astride the great horse Thunder, silently greeting passersby from the sidewalk.

She gives Cowboy Craig a wave as she turns around the square, the statue of a Union Soldier standing guard at the edge of the park on her left, the Majestic Theater on her right. Seeing the "Mighty Majestic" evokes memories of lingering kisses and urgent breath, the smell of popcorn, and the disgusting glop that always made their shoes stick when they walked back out into the lobby.

The marquee announces this week's feature. A permanent wooden sign over the box office still says "Shows Friday and Saturday night, 7:00 and 9:00," an anachronism in the day of the three-hour feature film.

She suffers another sneezing attack and pulls over to the side of the road in front of Jill's Quilts until she's able to drive again. A car passes by slowly, and its driver, a middle-aged woman, stares at her. Mo pulls back onto the road and makes another left turn. The Courthouse Square is still on her left, and Sturdevant's ancient auto dealership stands like a fortress on her right, with its stone arch entryway and huge picture window. The old Studebaker sign still hangs above the door, although the logos in the window are for Honda, Acura, and Lexus.

At the four-way stop, she has planned to turn right, back onto Main and out of town, but another violent sneezing attack prompts her to turn left instead and drive back toward the pharmacy. The proud old Pentagram building dominates the fourth side of the square, with its historical marker commemorating founding editor, "Fighting Freddie" Fitzhugh. The sign in the window of Profitt's Ace Hardware still boasts of "The Farm Implements and Toys Museum" inside. Three men in overalls and seed caps sit on the bench outside Bev's Diner, solving the world's problems.

She finds a parking space in front of Wallace's. As she gets out of the car, a woman with black hair, obviously dyed, walks by, turns, and stares at her.

"Hello?" Mo says, but the woman turns away and keeps walking.

Downtown feels like a huge museum, or perhaps a movie set for the film of her childhood, and this feeling becomes stronger as she enters Wallace's. The wooden floor creeks under her feet as she walks down the wide aisle between shelves holding—she would almost swear to it—the same dusty nostrums that were there when she left to go to college 20 years before.

Pain relievers and such are right where she knew they'd be, at the back of the store, but gone are the cages filled with live birds, and the soda fountain looks to have been closed for some time. The high counter—behind which Mr. Wallace once filled the town's prescriptions and kept its secrets—seems unmanned just now.

She scours the shelves but fails to find any sort of antihistamine she recognizes, so she walks to the front, past a stand-up display of sunglasses. A thin teenage girl with brunette hair pulled back in a ponytail leans against the glass counter, reading a movie magazine. She looks up and does a classic double take.

"Did you change your hair or something?"

"Did I . . .?" Mo pats at her hair reflexively. "Oh! You must know Maddie."

The girl studies her in earnest now. "God, you look just like her! Except her hair's different. And you're thinner. Are you, like, twins or something?"

"Yep. My name's Monona. I grew up here."

"You're her!" The girl's eyes widen. "You're famous!"

"Hardly." Mo smiles despite herself. "What's your name?"

"Janice." Her eyes widen again. "You're here because of Aidan! It's on the front page and everything. I bet anything he didn't do it."

"You know Aidan?"

"We go to school together. We're both seniors. So you're, like, his aunt, huh?"

"Just like it."

"That's really freaky. I mean, being a twin. I used to wish I had a twin, growing up. Do you guys have, like, that telepathy thing twins get?"

"Sometimes. I don't seem to be able to find the antihistamines."

"You want the kind that relieves sneezing, itching, blowing, and runny nose for 12 hours without causing drowsiness," she asks, grinning, "or the one that's got your name on the package?"

"Any national brand will be fine."

The girl bends behind the counter and emerges with a package. "These do?"

"Those are fine." Mo takes her wallet from her purse.

"I need to see your driver's license."

"I'm paying cash."

"I still have to check ID. You have to sign the register thingee, too."

"Why's that?"

"It's got that stuff in it. Pseudowhatchamacallit. The stuff they make meth with."

Mo fishes her driver's license from her billfold and sets it on the counter. Janice brings a spiral notebook from under the counter, opens to a page near the front already half-filled with entries in ink, and prints Mo's name, address, and license number.

"You need to sign it," she says, turning the notebook toward Mo. "Right there."

Mo scans the rest of the page, looking for familiar names. She signs, and Janice replaces the notebook below the counter.

"Anything else?" Janice asks automatically, back in clerk mode now.

"No. Yes. Just a minute."

Mo circles the counter to a low shelf holding stacks of *The Des Moines Register, USA TODAY,* and *The Pentagram.* She takes copies of all three papers and brings them to the register, and Janice scans them in.

"That it?"

"For now."

Janice hits a key, and the computer whirs, spitting out a long slip of paper. "Tell Aidan I said 'hey.'" She tears off the tongue of paper and hands it to Mo.

"I sure will." Mo counts out exact change.

"You going to be here for awhile?"

Mo realizes she has no idea how long she might be staying. "Awhile," she says.

"Well, see ya, then."

"Yeah. See ya. Nice meeting you, Janice."

"Me, too. You're my first celebrity."

Mo laughs but can think of nothing to say to that.

The sun has dropped below the buildings across the square. The oak trees in the park cast long, pale shadows in the waning light. Mo fans open *The Pentagram.*

COWBOY LINEMAN SUSPENDED IN DRUG BUST
Won't Be Eligible for Division Semi Game Friday

Now, there's an editor who really has his priorities in order. A kid's future is at stake, and we're worried about a football game. She folds the papers and tosses them into the car before getting in herself. She now has only 12 miles of very familiar road to traverse to reach the farm, her past, and whatever the immediate future might bring.

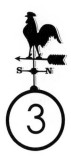

3

Mo and Maddie clear away the dinner dishes and stand side by side at the double sink, Maddie washing, Mo rinsing and drying. Danny scurries to put the dry dishes away.

"Are you coming to my magic show, Auntie Mo?"

"Of course! I drove all this way just to see it."

"No, you didn't," Danny says, half-believing. "Where does this go, Mom?"

He holds up the big serving platter that has recently held roast beef, roasted red potatoes, and mixed vegetables. With the scratch buttermilk biscuits and fresh, homemade apple pie, it had been a feast for the four of them.

Grammy Quinn sits in her rocker in the living room, listening to the radio. Aidan, free on signature bond after a night in the county jail, has yet to appear from the loft in the barn he now claims as his space.

"I'm going to do the ring trick. I can show you how to do it if you want."

"Why don't you save it so she'll be surprised at the show?" Maddie suggests.

"Aw, Mom."

"A real magician never reveals his secrets," Mo tells him.

"Really?"

"Ask any magician."

"Tell Auntie Mo about the other magician who'll be performing," Maddie urges.

"Oh, yeah! Fondue the Magician!"

"I think it's 'Shaundu,' honey. The platter goes in the cabinet in the dining room. And then I want you to do your homework. Your Aunt Mo and I can finish these."

"Aw, Mom!"

"I caught this guy's act four times when the twins were going to St. Pete's," Maddie tells Mo as Danny walks away. "He's actually very good."

"What's that magician's name again, Mama?" Danny asks from the doorway.

"Homework," Maddie says.

"Okay."

His feet thunder on the stairs.

"Danny seems to be handling everything well," Mo says.

"I don't think it's really sunk in yet. Maybe not for any of us."

"You missed a spot." Mo hands a dessert plate back.

"Can't you just dry a little harder?"

Maddie rewashes the plate and then submerges the roasting pan in the sudsy water and wipes her hands on her apron.

"Let's let that soak," she says.

"Suits me."

"How about a walk?"

"Yeah!" Danny says from the stair landing.

"I thought you were doing homework!"

"I can finish when we get back. I don't have much."

"Have you done your math?"

"Not yet. It's not too hard tonight."

"Okay. Go see if Grammy Quinn wants to come."

His sneakers slap the floor as he charges through the dining room.

"His father used to go over his math homework with him every night," Maddie says, hanging the apron on its hook. "I'm afraid I'm not much help in that department."

"He looks so much like Kenny."

"Doesn't he? He's his dad all over again."

The thundering sneakers return. "She says she'll just listen to the radio. Can Chance come?"

"Sure."

"Okay!"

Danny shoots out the back door.

"Danny! Door."

The door slams. Mo watches from the window as her nephew races down the dirt driveway.

"You might need a sweater," Maddie says. "The evenings are getting a chill to them."

"Who's Chance?" Mo asks when they are outside, walking side by side down the long driveway, their paces perfectly matched.

"The Logan's youngest boy. He's just Danny's age, which works out great, except he goes to the public, so they don't see each other during the day.

"And when you get Chance, you also get Wrecker, the Logan family mutt. He's allegedly a purebred Golden, but I think a panther must have jumped the fence."

"How are the Logans working out?"

"Great. They have three boys. Chance, Mark, who's 11, and Matthew, who's 13. They're good kids."

"Matthew, Mark, and Chance? What happened to Luke?"

A gangly dog turns in at the driveway and charges them, woofing happily.

"Stand by to repel borders," Maddie says, and Mo smiles at their father's expression.

The dog bounds straight to Maddie and jumps up, nearly knocking her over with his big paws on her shoulders. She roughs the fur behind his ears with both hands.

"Off," she says quietly.

Wrecker drops to all fours and turns to Mo, smelling her shoes with keen interest.

"He doesn't want jump up on me?" Mo asks.

"I warned him that you know karate."

Mo laughs. "I doubt my defense training would work on this guy."

"Sit!" Maddie says sternly.

The dog's hind end hits the dirt.

"Down," Maddie says, holding her hand out, palm down.

The dog creeps into a lying-down position, his eyes on Maddie.

"That's amazing!" Mo says.

"He was easy to train. He's a real pleaser, this one. Aren't you, boy?"

Wrecker's tail pounds the dirt.

"Watch this."

Maddie digs into the pocket of her housedress. Wrecker watches intently, muscles tense, eyes following her hand as it emerges from the pocket. Maddie bends down and carefully places a small, dumbbell-shaped object on the dog's muzzle.

"Stay," Maddie says firmly.

Wrecker watches her, his tail swishing slowly from side to side, the rest of his body unmoving.

"Okay!" Maddie says.

Wrecker shakes his head, catching the treat in the air and crunching it with his teeth.

"Good boy!"

"That really is remarkable."

"Okay!" Maddie says, and Wrecker leaps up and gallops down the driveway, circling back to make sure they're following.

They reach the end of the driveway and turn left onto Durning-Quinn Road.

A drainage ditch runs alongside the road, a sliver of water in the bottom.

Three feet back from the ditch, a wooden lattice fence, recently painted white, marks the property line.

Wrecker trots ahead. Maddie stoops to pick up a beer can, turns it upside down to shake out the moisture, flattens it in her hands, and slips it into her sweater pocket. A rabbit bolts across the road, and Wrecker accelerates into a full gallop, veering into the ditch after his prey.

"Wrecker! Stop!"

The dog freezes in mid-stride, turns, and sits, watching her.

"Wow!" Mo says. "I wouldn't have believed it if I hadn't seen it."

"That's the hardest thing to teach a dog. Wrecker! Come!"

Wrecker gallops up and sits, looking expectantly at Maddie, who digs another treat out of her pocket.

She hands the biscuit to Mo. "You give it to him."

Mo holds out the biscuit tentatively. Wrecker looks at Maddie.

"It's okay!"

Tail wagging, Wrecker sidles up to Mo.

"Gentle lips," Maddie instructs.

Wrecker leans forward and slurps down the biscuit, his mouth soft and wet on Mo's fingers. He turns and ambles back up the road, the rabbit apparently forgotten.

"I didn't feel any teeth."

"Everett, Mr. Logan, is training him to retrieve ducks. He has to learn to carry them without his teeth puncturing them."

They turn onto Cemetery Ridge Road, which T's from the left into Durning-Quinn Road. The white fence marking the Durning property line is still on their left. On the other side of the road, another wooden fence, its paint peeling and faded, marks Quinn property. On the right, 100 yards up, a narrow, dirt driveway leads up a gentle slope past a white-frame two-story house. A window box sports a row of geraniums, past blossoming but still robust. A dirty, red pickup truck sits in the driveway next to the house. A rope swing dangles to the ground from one of the high branches of a nearby maple, and the start of a tree house nestles in the branches seven or eight feet off the ground.

Danny charges around the corner of the house, followed closely by another boy, taller and heavier than Danny, with a thatch of flaming red hair.

Wrecker is right behind him. Spotting them, Danny skids to a stop and waves, and the other boy piles into him.

"Hello!" Mo calls, waving back.

Danny looks at the other boy and, as if by some signal, they pivot and run back behind the house, giggling fiercely. Wrecker bounds after them with joyful yelps.

"The old place looks good," Mo says.

"The Logans take real good care of it. I'd sure rather have a nice family like them living in it than to have it sit vacant. A house falls apart fast when there's nobody in it."

"Mom seems good, too."

"She has good days and bad. I think she hurts worse than she lets on."

A larger version of the red-haired boy walks out onto the porch of the house as Mo and Maddie draw even with it on the road.

"Hello, Mrs. Durning," the boy calls down. "How are you?"

"Hi, Mark. I'm fine, thanks. Think we'll win Friday?"

"You bet!" He looks from Maddie to Mo, his perplexity showing on his face.

"This is my sister," Maddie says. "Mo, this is Mark Logan."

"Nice to meet you, Mark."

"It's very nice to meet you, ma'am." He shakes his head, grinning. "And folks say me and my brothers look alike."

"We've been told there's a slight family resemblance."

Mark forces a grin at the adults' joke. "Well, Pa's expecting me in the barn."

"The chores never end, do they?" Maddie notes.

"Not hardly. Nice to meet you." He vaults the porch railing and hits the ground running, slapping the side of the pickup as he lopes by.

Another 75 yards up, where the road crests gently, a metal archway marks the entrance to the shared family cemetery, where generations of Durnings and Quinns are buried. They turn in and walk the uneven dirt path between rows of tombstones.

Mo veers right and walks diagonally up the slope to the far southwest corner of the cemetery where, shaded by a huge maple just off the cemetery grounds, a double tombstone bears two names:

JAMES PETER QUINN

   b December 25, 1947

   d September 3, 1985

and next to it:

EILEEN COONEY QUINN

b July 21, 1941

The tombstone includes a cross, the inscription "I am the way and the life," and a flower holder filled with geraniums. Mo kneels at the foot of the grave and prays silently for several minutes. When she stands, Maddie puts an arm over her shoulder, and they walk together along the back fence.

"There's a new one," Mo notes.

"Mr. Averbach. Remember? He taught music at the high school."

"I do remember! He was a nice man. But he isn't family, is he?"

"He had AIDS. He didn't have anyplace else, or any family."

They approach the new grave near the wire fence marking the back of the cemetery. The mounded dirt is still dark. Down the slope, a creek winds through a stand of birches.

"The tombstone was supposed to be here last week. Most of the town turned out for the funeral."

"How sad."

"Isn't it! I can't imagine not being close to your family." She slips an arm around Mo's waist and hugs her, so that their hips bump. "Thank you so much for being here."

"Of course I'm here."

The sun is already setting, and black clouds have rolled in from the west.

"Aidan hasn't said three words since I drove him home. I have no idea what's going on with him. It's like I don't know him anymore."

"Our sweet Aidan is still in there somewhere."

"I can't believe he's mixed up with drugs."

"He's a good kid, Maddie. We'll get this straightened out."

"I wish Kenny were here!"

"I do too, honey."

"Coach kicked Aidan off the team, of course. He had to."

"Just when they're finally going to the playoffs."

"The sad thing is, Aidan was really feeling like he'd been accepted by his teammates. Rick Sherman himself came by the house last week."

"Who?"

"Sorry. I forget sometimes that you don't live here. Rick's the star quarterback. Coach says he's got a good shot at the pros if he doesn't get hurt. He's a four-sport letterman, Mr. All-Everything."

"I think I just felt a drop."

"We'd better head back."

Danny and Chance race up, Wrecker close behind, as Mo and Maddie reach the cemetery gate. "It's gonna rain, Mom!" Danny shouts. "We'd better hurry!"

"Come here, Wrecker!" Maddie says as the dog starts to head into the culvert.

He trots up to her and sits.

"Heel!"

She starts down the road, Wrecker on her left, his eyes on her.

"I can make him heel, too," Chance says.

"Now if we could just train him to milk the cows, huh?" Maddie says. "You want to try it?" she asks Mo.

"Do you really think he'd obey me? You were always better with the family dogs."

"He'd better, if he knows what's good for him."

"Yeah!" Chance says. "He'd better!"

"Stop!" Maddie says. "Sit!"

The dog instantly obeys.

A cold, fat raindrop hits Mo on the tip of her nose.

"Tell him to heel and slap your left hip."

"Heel?"

"Say it like you mean it."

"Heel!"

The dog looks from Maddie to Mo and slides in next to Mo.

"How fast should I walk?"

"You set the pace."

She starts down the road and is amazed to see that Wrecker sticks with her. "Maybe he thinks I'm you," she says.

"He can tell us apart by our smells. Even identical twins can't fool that nose."

Wrecker heels all the way to the Quinn driveway, where Maddie releases him, and he and Chance run up toward their house.

"See ya!" Danny calls after them.

"See ya!" Chance answers without looking back.

Mo sees a flash out of the corner of her eye.

"One thousand one, one thousand two," Maddie counts softly, "one thousand—"

Thunder rumbles across the sky to the right. As if waiting for this cue, the skies open, an instant downpour. Laughing and turning his face to the rain, Danny runs ahead.

"We might as well walk," Maddie says. "We're already as wet as we're going to get."

Their mother has already gone to bed by the time they get back inside and dry off. Maddie sends Danny upstairs to take his bath and finish his homework and puts on water to boil. She and Mo sit in the living room, drinking cocoa and watching the storm make its slow way west, forks of lightning snaking the sky, the thunder a distant, throaty rumble.

"Sorry about the soaking," Maddie says. "I don't think they predicted this one."

"Don't be sorry! I liked it."

Maddie smiles. "I remember something you told Mom once when she wanted you to wear a raincoat to school. Remember those ugly yellow things she bought for us?"

"I hated it! I thought it made me look like a big, fat bee."

"Do you remember what you said?"

Mo shakes her head.

"She said we had to have a plan for if it rained."

"That's Mom, all right."

"And you said you did have a plan. I think you even called it a 'contingency plan.' We were only in, like, fourth grade, but you were always using words like that. Dad called you his 'little professor.'"

"I remember that. But I don't remember my 'contingency plan.' What was it?"

"'If it rains, I'll get wet.' That's what you said."

"What kind of a plan is that?"

"Don't look at me! It was your plan. Mom just stared at you like you'd lost your mind, and then she started laughing."

"Did she make me wear the raincoat?"

"Of course not. She always let you have your way."

"She did not! Did it rain that day?"

"I don't remember."

Mo hears a rustling on the stair landing and turns to see a swatch of blue disappear behind the corner.

"Danny," Maddie says sternly.

Danny appears on the landing, wearing Batman pajamas. "I'm done with my homework."

"Did you brush your teeth?"

"Uh-huh."

"Did you brush *all* of them?"

"Every one. Aunt Mo, will you tuck me in?"

"Of course I will."

"Don't let him con you," Maddie cautions as Mo stands. "He's got a million stall tactics."

Danny leads his aunt by the hand up the stairs to his room, which, although filled with the details of a boy's life, is neat and orderly. Books are stacked on the desk next to a framed picture of the family, which must have been taken shortly before Kenny shipped out. Posters on the wall depict military fighter planes and choppers and scenes from football games. Several model airplanes dangle on wires from the ceiling.

"Can I show you my trick?"

"Of course you can."

Mo sits on the bed as Danny literally hops over to the closet, emerging a moment later with three large rings in his right hand.

"Watch," he says, grinning.

His tongue sticking out of the corner of his mouth, he drops one of the rings to the floor, holds a ring in each hand, and bangs them together, making a dull clunk. Frowning, he examines the rings, turning one in his hand. After a moment, he straightens.

"Watch," he says again.

Another clunk.

"It's not working! They're supposed to link."

"Well, first you need a little patter."

"What's patter?"

"It's your spiel. Chit-chat to distract your audience."

"I don't know any patter."

"Why don't you start by showing us that there's nothing up your sleeves. Remember? Like on Rocky and Bullwinkle?"

"What's Rocky and Boywrinkle?"

"Never mind. Just a cartoon your ancient auntie used to watch."

"Can you show me?"

He thrusts the rings out toward her.

"Sure," she says, standing to accept the rings. "You sit down and be the audience."

"Okay."

He sits on folded legs on the edge of the bed, and Mo stands a few feet in front of him.

"Ladies and gentlemen, boys and girls, children of all ages," Mo says, sweeping the room with her eyes as if addressing a huge arena, "I am about to perform a trick that will amaze and astound you."

Danny giggles.

"Please notice at no time do my fingers leave my hands."

She wiggles her fingers at Danny, who giggles again.

"Please notice, also, that I have nothing whatsoever up my sleeves." She dramatically pulls on her sweater cuffs. "Except, of course, my arms."

"That's silly."

"That's the idea. Ladies and gentlemen, boys and girls, children of all ages, I will now attempt to do the impossible, linking these two solid rings.

"Which, of course, I don't actually know how to do."

"I'll show you." Danny hops up and takes the rings.

"No! A magician never reveals his tricks! You go ahead and amaze and astound me."

They exchange places. Grinning, Danny holds the rings up. "Ladies and gentlemen of all ages . . . No! I goofed."

"The exact words don't matter. Keep going. Show me your sleeves."

"Oh, yeah."

"What are you two kids doing up there?" Maddie calls from downstairs.

"Just a minute, Mom!" Danny shouts. "I'm learning how to patter."

"You're what?"

"I'll be down in a minute, Sis," Mo calls.

Mo has Danny run through the trick successfully three times, including the beginnings of some patter, then tucks him in and kisses him on the forehead.

"Thanks for teaching me patter."

"You're welcome, Tiger. Keep practicing until you don't even have to think about it."

"I love you, Aunt Mo."

"I love you, too, sweetheart."

Back downstairs, Mo sits again with Maddie in the living room, and they talk of Aidan's run-in with the law, of Kenny off fighting in Iraq, of their mother's crippling rheumatoid arthritis and frequent confusion, and of the precarious farm finances.

"I'm so sorry, Sis," Mo says at last. "You've got an awful lot on your plate."

"Oh, the plate runneth over, all right. But still, we have so much to be thankful for. And I'm so looking forward to Eileen coming home for Thanksgiving. I miss her even more than I thought I would."

"She's still loving G.W.?"

"By all accounts. She says her dormitory is two blocks from the White House. Can you imagine?"

"I really can't."

Maddie pats her sister's leg. "I've been going on and on," she says. "What about you? How's life in Mitchell?"

"Well, we haven't had a murder for two whole months."

"I still can't get over that! Two murders in three months! And you caught both killers!"

"I didn't catch them."

"You did so! And you had to use karate to fight off that awful man, or he would have killed you, too!"

"It's not karate, Sis. It's just self-defense training."

"Whatever it is, you're all the talk at Bev's."

"I find that hard to believe, with the Cowboys playing for the championship."

"Well, okay. There is some football talk, I admit. But you're still a hero around here."

Mo shrugs and sips her cocoa. "I don't feel very heroic," she says.

After a long silence, Maddie asks, "How are things with you and Doug?"

"Not good. He said he couldn't promise he'd be there when I got back."

"Oh, honey!"

"I'm going to try to call him before I go to bed."

"Things will work out. You and Doug love each other."

"We argue."

"Of course you do. All married couples argue."

"We argue a lot. He resents the hours I put in at the paper." She sighs. "'The course of true love ne'er runs smooth.' Isn't that what Dad always used to tell us when one of us was broken-hearted over some boy?"

"I remember."

"I always thought he made it up until I took Shakespeare in college."

"He was a good man," Maddie says.

"Shakespeare?"

Maddie pokes her. "I meant Dad, and you know it."

"He was the best."

"To Dad," she says, hoisting her mug.

"To Dad," Mo echoes. "And so to bed."

"Me, too. Big doings tomorrow."

They stand.

"You're in Aidan's room," Maddie says, "if that's okay."

"That's fine. You don't have to show me the way."

"I'd better explain about the upstairs bathroom."

"As long as it flushes."

"Of course it flushes! But it's such a mess. Kenny was halfway through fixing it up when his unit got called up."

"I'll manage fine."

"There's an extra blanket on the shelf in the closet if you need it."

"Thanks."

"I hope the posters don't give you nightmares. Aidan's out of his heavy metal stage, now, thank God, but he hasn't taken down those awful posters."

"I'll say a rosary to ward off the evil spirits."

Maddie laughs. "If you need anything, just holler."

"Thanks, Sis. I'll be fine."

"Aidan's got an Internet connection, if you want to use it."

"How things have changed down on the farm, huh?"

"We're really quite up-to-date. You have to be to survive."

They embrace, and when they step apart, Mo sees that Maddie is crying.

"It's going to be alright, Sis."

"I know." Maddie swipes at the tears. "Now that my big sister is here."

"Believe it!"

As Mo pads softly upstairs, she wishes she felt as confident as she hopes she sounded. Aidan probably won't face severe penalties for a first-offense drug possession charge, but Mo can see the strain this latest complication has placed on her sister, on top of an already difficult and stressful life.

As she hoists her suitcase onto the bed and fishes out her nightgown and toiletries, she feels a pang of guilt. Maddie stayed behind when Mo went off to college, and she's still taking care of Mom and the farms—legacy and livelihood for two families.

Maddie wasn't kidding about the posters. Fierce, demonic faces glare down from the walls. Bare-chested bodies, glistening with sweat, seem to twist and writhe. These guys must be playing the soundtrack in hell, Mo decides.

She snaps open her cell phone and punches in her home number on speed dial. With a surge of longing, she imagines the phone ringing in the kitchen, sees Doug striding through the living room, frowning at the interruption.

After five rings, she hears her own voice. "You've reached the home of Monona Quinn and Douglas Stennett. We can't come to the phone right now, but if you'll leave a message, we'll get back to you."

"Doug? It's me. I wanted to let you know I got here safe. I don't have much to report yet. Maddie seems to be bearing up well, considering. I plan to talk to the sheriff in the morning. Just wanted to make sure everything's all right. I—I love you."

She *hates* talking to an answering machine. She snaps the cell shut and tosses it on the bed. The computer sitting on

Aidan's desk tempts her. She could answer emails, go over page layouts, even write her column for the next week's edition. But all that seems very far away, and a relentless weariness penetrates to her bones.

She picks up the small, cloth kit containing her personals and pads down the hall to the bathroom, guided by the night-light in Danny's bedroom. She pauses at his open doorway to watch him sleep, curled in his bed, one leg sticking out from the covers.

Dear God, watch over and protect him, she prays, and guide his path in righteousness.

She has to grope the wall until she finds the switch in the bathroom, and when she clicks it on, she gets a shock. A hole gapes in the far wall, next to the shower stall. The walls have been stripped and about half the surface sanded. A grate has been removed from the ceiling, and the whirring of the fan sounds like the wailing of a demented banshee.

A Superman comic book lies open, face down on the floor next to the toilet; for want of anything else, Mo picks it up and reads while she sits.

The noise of the fan is truly unnerving. Under the metallic whirring, she could swear she hears a thumping and even the murmuring of voices. She clicks off the switch, plunging the room into darkness and a silence made more absolute by the noise that preceded it. Nothing. The old farmhouse is quiet, save for the breeze, the last of the sudden storm, stirring the trees outside. A branch creaks.

She turns on the light and fan, and the strange sounds bubble up again, a coven of witches surrounding their cauldron.

Back in Aidan's room, she tries to call Doug again, this time breaking the connection after five rings. When she turns out the overhead light, the darkness is total and stunning. She climbs gratefully under the covers, but, as tired as she is, she lies sleepless, missing Doug, wondering where he is, aching in sympathy for her sister.

Dear Lord, she prays, I have to turn all this over to you and trust you to take care of things. It's way more than I can handle. She prays the rosary, counting off the prayers on her fingers, and midway through the third decade, with the chimes from the grandfather clock downstairs tolling midnight, she falls into blessed sleep.

4

"Superman and Lois Lane are married?"

"I know! Isn't it gross?"

Mo and Danny sit at the kitchen table, while Maddie works with her back to them at the stove. There are four places set, and a vase holds fresh wildflowers, the last of the season. Mo has pulled on jeans and a solid black T-shirt, with a "Madison Mavericks" sweatshirt over that. Danny is wearing his Boy Scout uniform, complete with merit badge sash. Mo sips from a mug of hot coffee.

"Did Aidan's posters give you nightmares?" Maddie asks without turning.

"No. I slept fine. I will admit I was a little unnerved when I opened my eyes this morning and the first thing I saw was somebody spitting fire at me."

Maddie laughs. "Did your allergies calm down?"

"Yeah. The meds seem to have done the trick. That probably explains why I slept so soundly, too. I'm still a little groggy. Hey, since when do you have to show ID to buy allergy medication?"

"Since about six months ago, I think. State law."

"Why?"

"They use it to make methamedamenes," Danny says.

"Methamphetamines." Mo nods. "Right. The clerk did mention that. For a minute, she thought I was you, by the way," she adds to her sister.

"Who? Janice?"

"It's real bad," Danny says. "It makes you do crazy things, and you can even die! Mom, where's Grammy?"

"Still sleeping," Maddie says.

"She was always up before anybody else," Mo says.

"She's not sleeping well at night. I hear her get up a lot. So I'm glad for whenever she can get some rest.

"Here you are," she adds, sliding a plate in front of her sister. "Farmer's omelet, made by a genuine farmer."

"I can't eat all that!"

Maddie serves Danny scrambled eggs and toast spread thick with peanut butter.

"Have you had a lot of problems with meth around here?" Mo asks.

"The sheriff thinks there's a lab in the area, but they haven't been able to find it. Isn't that something? I always thought drugs were a big-city problem. And now my own son . . ." She takes a deep breath.

"I don't like Superman any more," Danny says.

"You don't?"

"Let's say grace first, honey" Maddie says, stopping Danny's forkful of eggs inches from his mouth. She wipes her hands on her apron and, standing between them, takes Mo and Danny by the hand. "Why don't you offer grace, Danny?" she says.

"Good Lord, look down upon us now . . ."

"Not that one."

"Bless us oh Lord and these Thy gifts which we are about to receive amen."

"Amen," Maddie says, squeezing Mo's hand, and Mo murmurs "Amen."

"Can we see a movie?" Danny asks around a mouthful of egg.

"We're going to see a movie with the school, remember?"

"Oh, yeah! Can you come with us, Auntie Mo? It's at the Majestic!"

Maddie joins them at the table, carrying her plate, which holds an omelet. "They're having a special showing of *The Sound of Music* for the school kids."

"I'd love to come, honey," Mo tells Danny.

All three look up as the back door swings open, and a tall, muscular young man with short, blond hair walks in, shoulders hunched, head down.

"Hi, Aidan!" Danny shouts out.

"Whassup, little bro?" Aidan tousles Danny's hair.

"Whassup?" Danny says, and giggles.

"I can make you an omelet," Maddie says. "I've got everything ready."

"That's okay. Hi, Aunt Mo. When'd you get here?"

"Yesterday afternoon. How are you, Aidan?"

He shrugs and shuffles to the cupboard, pulls down a box of cinnamon toast cereal, pours some into a cup, and, still standing, takes a handful and puts it into his mouth.

"For heaven's sake, sit down," Maddie says. "Use a spoon. Have some milk with that."

"Gotta go," he says, taking the cup. "You want a ride, squirt?"

"Yeah!" Danny jumps up.

"Finish your breakfast," Maddie says. "I can take him," she adds to Aidan.

"I'll drop him off. It's right on the way. I gotta be there early."

"Why is that?"

Aidan looks away. "McSweeney said he wants to talk to me before first period."

"*Mr.* McSweeney. Did he say what about?"

"You *know* what *Mr.* McSweeney wants to talk about. Come on, doofus," he says to Danny. "You'll never earn any merit badges sitting there."

"Take your toast with you," Maddie says as Danny bounces up, comes around the table, and throws his arms around Mo's neck.

"I love you, Aunt Mo." He squeezes her so hard something pops in her shoulder.

"I love you, too, honey," she says, awkwardly returning the hug while still seated.

"See you later," Aidan says. "Good to see you, Aunt Mo."

"Good to see you, too, Aidan."

"Are you coming with us to the game tonight?" Maddie asks him.

Aidan stops, his hand on the doorknob. Danny, backpack slung over his shoulder and peanut butter toast in hand, stands behind him. Aidan shakes his head twice. "Bye," he says, and the door slams shut behind them.

Maddie's fork clatters on her plate, and she pushes away from the table.

"I'll clean up," she says. "I'm due at the store in 45 minutes."

"I'll do it. Finish your breakfast."

"That's okay. I'm fine."

Maddie carries her plate to the counter and scrapes her omelet into the garbage.

Mo approaches her, puts her hands on her sister's shoulders, and squeezes gently. Maddie puts a hand on top of Mo's. She sobs quietly, while Mo gently kneads her shoulders.

"I can't even talk to him anymore," she manages.

"You're going to get through this."

"Now that you're here, I fall apart."

"You're not falling apart. You're entitled to a good cry."

"Did you talk to Doug last night?"

"No. He didn't pick up."

"Maybe he was asleep."

"Maybe. He didn't answer this morning, either."

"Listen, you want to come into town with me? We could have lunch. Oh, wait. I can't. I'm working at the soup kitchen today."

"You work at a soup kitchen?"

"I volunteer once a week. Actually, I shouldn't call it that. Luke hates that term."

"Luke?"

"Luke Clausen. He runs the program."

"Could you use an extra hand?"

"That would be great."

"Where is it? I'll meet you there."

"Basement of the Lutheran Church. Behind the Majestic. We start setting up at 11:00. The meal is at noon."

"Great. It'll just take me a minute to get ready, and I'll ride in with you. Will Mom be all right? I mean, if nobody's here when she wakes up?"

"She'll be fine. Mr. Logan looks in on her. She hates it if she thinks he's keeping an eye on her. She's pretty fierce about wanting to be independent."

"Always was. I'll be ready in two shakes. What was that blessing you didn't want Danny to give?"

Her sister laughs. "It's something Kenny taught him. I think he picked it up in the Guard. 'Good Lord, look down upon us now, and see that we're not forgotten. Give us food that's fit to eat, for this is surely rotten. One spud for the four of us. Thank God, there are no more of us. Amen.'"

They laugh together.

"So, what are you going to do until 11:00?" Maddie asks when they are on their way to town in her Chevy pickup. "I'm afraid the shopping is rather limited."

"I'm not real big on shopping anyway. I thought I might see if I could talk with the sheriff." She catches Maddie's quick glance. "What? Do I need an appointment?"

The fields are full of the stubble from the season's corn crop. The Garrison's pumpkin patch is picked clean, the withered vines waiting to be plowed under.

"I don't know whether to tell you or let it be a surprise."

"Tell me what? What's the big mystery?"

"Todd Brabender's the sheriff now."

"Todd . . . I thought he went off to Indiana or Illinois and joined the police force."

"He did. Fort Wayne. He came back home. He was Sheriff Possun's deputy for three years, and when Possun retired, we elected Todd. We would have elected him governor after he quarterbacked us to the state finals."

"Is he a good sheriff?"

"You used to think he was good at a lot of things."

Mo swats her sister on the arm. "That was a long time ago," she says.

"Ain't that the truth? And yes, he's a fine sheriff, although this drug business has got him buffaloed. Guess who his top deputy is."

"Barney Fife."

"Close. Randall Lampere. He looks like somebody strapped a gun on a flagpole. But he does keep things organized."

"Todd would need help in that department, all right."

"Didn't he forget to write a speech when he was running for student body president?"

"He didn't forget. He just didn't bother."

"And won anyway, of course."

"In a landslide. The man could charm the stripes off a zebra."

"He certainly had that effect on you."

"That's enough of that!" Mo pokes her sister again, and they share another laugh.

"I'm so glad you're here. I don't think I've laughed in months."

They fall silent, and Mo has time to reflect on the man with whom she thought she was ready to spend a lifetime. Would he have aged much? Had she? That was a lifetime ago, she reminds herself. She's a very long way from high school now.

5

The Sheriff's office is a block north of the square, next to Evan's barbershop. ("If your hair isn't becoming to you, you should be coming to me.") And sure enough, there's Evan, sitting in the shop's lone barber chair, reading the morning *Register* and waiting for a customer. A glance through the window is enough to assure Mo that nothing has changed in the shop where Evan has been cutting the townsfolk's hair since before Mo was born. Probably the same *Field and Stream* magazines litter the table, and the same jars of Butch Wax and Wildroot line the shelf behind the chair.

This town is a museum, she thinks, but as she pauses at the sheriff's office door, she knows that things have changed. Comfortable, pot-bellied Norman Possun is gone; Todd Brabender, the high school hero, has come home to keep the peace.

She gives the doorknob a firm turn and enters.

As she takes in the large, sparsely furnished room, she realizes that she's been imagining Sheriff Andy Taylor's office in Mayberry, complete with Otis, the town drunk, in a jail cell.

Instead she sees an open, airy room with several desks and no sign of Otis or jail bars. Behind the desk closest to the door, a plump young woman sits typing, her computer making the trilling sound of a metallic brook. She has what looks to be a tiny diamond in one nostril and several small bands lacing each earlobe. Her broad, full lips and large, brown eyes make Mo think of a girl she knew in high school. What was her name? Nancy something.

Sitting at the desk nearest the back wall, a tall, thin man in khaki uniform hunches over a computer screen, his back to her. The other desks are unmanned.

"Help you?" the young lady says, her fingers still trilling the keyboard.

"I'm here to see Sheriff Brabender."

"You can just go on in." She nods toward the back of the room.

"Thanks."

Mo's loafers clack harshly on the smooth, bare wooden floor. The man at the computer seems absorbed in a U.S. Department of Labor Web site as she passes by. The door on the right is labeled RESTROOM with the sort of sign you buy off a rack at the hardware store. Taped to the other door, a computer printout announces in large, all-cap letters, SHERIFF TODD BRABENDER.

She taps lightly on the sheriff's door.

"Yep. Come on in."

The voice freezes her for a moment. She takes a deep breath and opens the door.

The office is small and cluttered, the walls covered with posters, maps, and a calendar. A window at the back of the room looks out on an alley and the back of another building. The battered old wooden desk holds more papers and books than it should, everything stacked in piles surrounding a computer that's at least 10 years old. A flat phone pad and receiver are almost lost in the stacks.

Todd Brabender sits behind the desk, arms crossed, head cocked, a grin playing at his lips. His light blue eyes burn holes in her. If he's surprised, he's handling it well.

"For months after I moved back here," he says, his deep voice soft and modulated, "every time I'd run into your sister, for just a second, I'd think it was you."

"You could always tell us apart in high school."

The smile reaches his eyes. "Still can," he says, standing. "You look wonderful."

His athlete's body is still lean, his khaki pants and shirt crisp and ironed. He lifts a thick, loose-leaf binder off the chair beside the desk, indicating that she should sit.

"Would you like coffee?"

"Yes, please."

"Excuse me."

He brushes past her, their bodies almost touching, and walks out into the common room, leaving the door open behind him. A police scanner crackles, and a tinny voice says something Mo can't understand. A phone rings; the young receptionist says, "Sheriff's Office."

He returns, leaving the door open behind him. He carries two Styrofoam cups, hands her one, and settles in behind his desk.

Black. He remembered.

"You were the only person I knew who drank coffee in high school," he says, smiling, his eyes steady on her.

"I could swear we went to high school with your receptionist," she says, taking a sip of the hot, bitter coffee.

His smile broadens. His eyes stay on her face. "Brace yourself. We went to school with her mother."

"Oh, God! Nancy something, right?"

"Nancy Hefty. She was Nancy Johnson for awhile. Now she's Nancy Hefty again. She works in Des Moines in an auto parts store, last I heard. Her daughter, Tiffany, stayed in town with her father to finish high school."

Mo shakes her head. "I haven't thought of Nancy Hefty in years."

He nods, still smiling, still watching her, still calm. "Is that coffee okay? It tastes pretty rancid to me. I think it's yesterday's."

"It's fine."

"I can make fresh."

"No, really. This is fine."

"So, you went off to the big city and became famous," he notes.

"Hardly famous."

"Page two columnist for the *Chicago Trib*? I'd call that famous. Mr. Clement was real proud of you."

"How is he? Do you ever see him?"

"He died two years ago. Diabetes."

"I'm sorry to hear it. Do you remember the swimming party he threw for the seniors?"

"How could I forget? I'd never see a guy with one leg do a cannonball!"

He shakes his head at the memory. "I didn't even know he was missing a limb until I saw him in a bathing suit."

"Neither did I," Mo admits, "and I was in his class for three years."

Todd slurps a little as he sips his coffee. "It's good to see you," he says. "You do look wonderful."

Mo feels herself blush. "Thank you, sir," she says. "Gallant as ever."

"The years have been more than kind to you."

"And to you," she says. "You look as if you could still quarterback the team to the state tourney."

He laughs. "It looks as if we might go back this year," he says. He takes a long swig of coffee. "Has the old town changed much?"

"Not really. I did get carded over at Wallace's for buying a decongestant. That's new."

"The druggies buy it to make meth."

"Isn't that like restricting the sale of paper because somebody could use it to roll a joint?"

"That's one way of looking at it. But we'd like to know if somebody tries to buy a carton of Sudafed. You have to figure that person's either got a hell of a nasal drip, or he's making a dangerous and illegal drug."

He sits up, folding his hands on the desk in front of him. He's not wearing a wedding ring. "How's Maddie doing? She puts on a brave face when I see her."

"She's a brave lady. She's had to be."

"Yes." He picks up his coffee cup, stares at it for a moment as if trying to remember where he's seen it before, and puts it down. "Do you remember Jackie Clark?"

"Leggy, busty, wasp-waisted, beautiful shoulder-length blond hair, head cheerleader her junior year? Can't say that I do. Whatever happened to her?"

"I married her. She was rebounding from Tommy Peters, and I was rebounding from you. It was a stormy 18 months."

"I'm sorry."

"No kids, thank God."

She feels herself searching for words before his steady, calm gaze.

"And you," he says. "You waited a long time before finding Mr. Right. A financial planner, I'm told by usually reliable sources. And the two of you moved to Wisconsin."

"Maddie never could keep a secret."

"I had to beat it out of her with a rubber hose."

"Not that it's a secret, of course."

"Of course."

He seems comfortable in the ensuing silence. She is decidedly not—but somehow can't figure out how to break it.

"Well." He leans back, lacing his hands behind his head. "I assume you came here to talk about Aidan."

"Yes."

He watches her, his gaze unwavering. A trickle of sweat slides under the collar of her blouse. He fishes a file folder from one of the piles on his desk, flips it open, and studies the single sheet of paper inside.

"It's a simple possession charge. The D.A. wants to charge him with intent to sell, but I don't think he can make it stick."

"Why would he want to be so hard on Aidan?"

"It isn't Aidan. The D.A.—Holleran is his name, and it couldn't be more appropriate—won the election with a 'zero tolerance' campaign. Sign of the times."

"What will happen?"

"For a first offense for possession, he should get probation." He closes the file and tosses it back on the desk. "That said, I think Maddie would be wise to get him a good attorney. He'll go before Judge Barrows in district court."

"He's a tough judge?"

"She. Very."

"I mentioned Lewis Crubb to Maddie."

Todd again leans back in his chair and laces his fingers behind his head.

"Good old Lewis," he says, smiling. "Remember when he talked Gassman out of giving us a pop quiz in social studies?"

"On the grounds that it violated six or seven of our Constitutional rights."

"Even Gassman had to smile."

The phone rings out in the commons.

"Line two, Deputy Lampere," Tiffany Johnston calls out.

"Sheriff's Office. Sheriff's Deputy Randall Lampere speaking. How may I serve you?"

Todd catches her eavesdropping. She catches him grinning.

"Hold on . . . Where? . . . Okay. And you discovered it was missing this morning? . . . Yeah . . . Yeah. Someone will be right out. Yeah . . . Okay . . . Yeah."

Deputy Lampere appears in the doorway. "We got another one, Sheriff. Excuse me," he adds, nodding toward Mo.

"Monona Quinn, this is Deputy Sheriff Randall Lampere, my good right hand. Deputy, perhaps you recognize this woman."

The tall, skinny young man squints, as if trying to bring her into focus.

Awareness dawns slowly. "You look a lot like Mrs. Durning," he says.

"Maddie and I are twins."

"Well, I'll be."

The Deputy continues to stare, as if the concept of identical twins is new to him.

"Deputy? The phone call?"

"What? Oh. Another theft."

"Who got hit this time?"

"Jake Richards. You want me to handle it?"

"I'll take it. I need to get out and stretch."

The way Deputy Lampere's face falls is almost comical.

"I need you to finish analyzing the data," Todd adds. "To give us a handle on the big picture."

The deputy's face brightens. "Right," he says. "Absolutely."

"Deputy Lampere is our big picture guy," Todd tells Mo. "Besides," he directs at the deputy, "don't you have to give a talk on drugs at the high school this afternoon?"

The Deputy straightens up, as if behind a podium, and clears his throat.

"Although marijuana remains the illicit drug of choice among youth," he says stiffly, "documented use of methamphetamines has risen sharply, especially in the upper grades. But two percent of Iowa children in the sixth grade admit to having used."

"That is shocking," Mo says.

The Deputy nods eagerly. "The Iowa Department of Corrections is leading the nation in the fight against illegal drugs," he tells her. "In August, 2000, we launched the Iowa Corrections Offender Network, ICON, and our Treatment Alternatives to Street Crime Management Information System, TASC, is the model for programs nationwide."

"Thank you, Deputy," Todd says.

"In 2002, the last year for which we have exact statistics, the Division of Narcotics Enforcement, State of Iowa, seized 120,000 grams of meth, with a street value of over $4 million. And that doesn't include cocaine, crack cocaine, ecstasy—"

"Thank you, Deputy!" Todd says again.

"Shouldn't I tell her about DEC?"

"Another time, Deputy. I think we'd both best attend to our duties now, don't you?"

"Right. Absolutely."

"It was nice meeting you, Deputy Lampere."

"Nice meeting you, Mrs . . ."

"Quinn. Monona Quinn."

The dawn again breaks behind the Deputy's guileless eyes. "You're the one who caught those two killers up in Wisconsin!"

Before Mo can respond, Deputy Lampere rushes to grab her hand and shake it roughly several times. "That was fine work!" he says. "Especially for a civilian!"

"Well, thank you, but . . ."

"It's an honor to meet you." He looks uncertainly toward the sheriff. "Is she here . . .?"

"She's here to visit family," Todd tells him.

"Right. Well . . ."

Deputy Lampere backs out of the room, carefully closing the door behind him.

"Believe it or not, he's actually a big help," Todd says. "I need someone like him to keep things organized. He fills out all the damn forms for the state. He actually seems to like it."

"I seem to remember you were never much for paperwork," Mo says.

Todd grins. "I'm kind of a big picture guy myself."

Mo laughs.

"I'd better head out to the Richards' place."

"What was stolen?"

"Fertilizer."

"Manure?"

"Liquid fertilizer contains anhydrous ammonia—liquid nitrogen. They use it to make meth by what they call the 'Nazi method.'"

"Why do they call it that?"

"I have no idea."

"It sounds dangerous."

"Extremely. They keep the nitrogen in those propane tanks from barbecue grills, coolers, all kinds of makeshift containers. If the stuff gets near your eyes, it can blind you. It burns the skin. The vapors can cause lung damage. You can even suffocate. If it leeches into the river, it kills the fish. I sound like Randy, making a speech."

He stands, and she takes that as her cue to get up.

"I'll walk you out," he says.

Randall Lampere is again working intently at his computer and doesn't seem to notice them as they walk by.

"I'm going out to the Richards," Todd tells Tiffany Johnston, who glances up from what looks to be a math textbook in her lap.

"'Kay," she says. "When shall I tell people you'll be back?"

"Tell them after lunch."

"Check."

Outside, they pause to stand on the walk in front of the sheriff's office.

"Perhaps we can continue our reminiscing when I get back? Lunch at Bev's, for old-time's sake?"

"I'd love to, but I'm meeting Maddie for lunch."

"Another time, then. How long are you staying?"

She shrugs. Sudden tears try to escape at the corners of her eyes.

He reaches out, puts the tips of his index and middle fingers lightly on her arm. "I know Aidan," he says softly, his kind eyes showing his concern. "I've been trying to keep an eye on him, with Kenny over in Iraq. He's going through some tough stuff, more than the usual growing pains of a smart kid coming into his manhood in a small town like this."

He looks left and right before continuing. Two women are standing and talking in front of Crosby's Apparel for All Seasons, three doors down. When he speaks again, his voice is even quieter. "I think Aidan's taking the fall for somebody. They can fool you, but this kid just isn't the druggie type. He's a good kid."

"I'm glad to hear you say that."

"You be sure to talk to Lewis."

"I will. Thanks again."

"You're welcome. You going to the game tonight?"

"Isn't everyone?"

"Just about. Maybe I'll see you there."

"Maybe."

She forces herself not to look back as she walks away. But she can't help wondering if he's looking at her and, if so, if he likes what he sees. Maybe they'll wind up sitting together at the game, she thinks. That would be a first. In the three years they dated in high school, she was always on the sidelines, watching the games, and he was always on the field, winning them.

Although it's a warm morning for early November, the shady park is deserted as she reaches the square. She turns right onto Church Street and heads west, spotting the spire of First Lutheran Church. A line has already formed by the side door adjacent to the parking lot. Mo quickens her pace. Not wanting to have to push her way to the front of the line to go in at the side door, she hurries around to the back, where a delivery van is parked in the alley, and volunteers are unloading the food other volunteers have donated and prepared.

As she rounds the building, she almost collides with a man.

"'Cuse me," he says in a rasping voice as he pushes past her.

She catches only a glimpse of him, enough to see that he's

wearing thick, dark glasses and a hat, the kind of hat men used to wear, a fedora.

Something impels her to turn and watch the man scuttle away. His long, heavy overcoat covers him like a shell; his shoulders are hunched, his head down. He looks, she decides, as if he's just stolen something and is making his getaway.

She's probably overreacting to a poor fellow down on his luck. She's been jumpy since her encounters with two killers in the space of three months, after all. He's no doubt harmless, she decides, as she walks to the truck to see if she can help carry in the food.

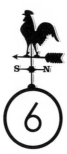

"There you are! I was about to send out a search party."

Maddie waves to her from across the room. Two stout older men grunt as they set up a table. Another man waits by a long cart holding dozens of metal folding chairs. In the back by the door to the kitchen, two women sit at a table, talking while they bundle knives, forks, and spoons into napkins and stack them on trays, each tray already holding eight plastic cups in two rows of four.

"I told folks you were coming," Maddie says, coming over to steer Mo by the elbow toward the back. "They can't wait to see you. Elsie Lamb especially."

Elsie Lamb! The name resonates. Such a good, patient woman. She'd seemed old even back when she suffered through five years of giving Mo private piano lessons every Wednesday afternoon in her parlor.

"You have such natural talent!" Elsie had told her many times. "Such a gift. But you just don't practice!"

It was true. Though piano came easily to her, Mo had little interest in playing and no interest at all in playing in front of a group at the dreaded twice-annual recitals. Maddie, on the other hand, wanted desperately to learn and practiced for at least an hour a day, but never made much progress.

"How was Todd?"

"Wipe that grin off your face. Todd was fine."

"I'll say he's fine. The man refuses to age."

"His deputy told me all about drug use among teenagers."

"Lectured you, you mean. And speaking of lecturing, here comes Luke."

A large man with a broad face topped by an unruly thatch of brown hair, bears down on them. He wears tattered sweat pants and a worn, brown T-shirt with faded lettering and logo, partially covered by an apron that has been laundered too many times. His grinning face glistens with sweat.

"Mo, this is Luke Clausen. He's the director of the hospital-ity program. Luke, this—"

"Yeah, yeah, yeah." He holds out a large, sweaty hand for shaking. "Geepers, you'd think you two were related or some-thing."

"We've been told there's a slight resemblance. What can I do to help?"

"Come with me."

Feeling like a dinghy in the wake of a battleship, Mo follows the giant to a large double-accordion door to their left. She has been in the basement once before, after the funeral of a high school classmate, Adrienne Walsh. Adrienne had been killed in a car crash that had left her boyfriend uninjured, at least physi-cally. Mo can't remember the boyfriend's name. Brian some-thing, maybe. He'd been drinking. He never came back to school. She'd heard he'd gotten his GED and gone to a trade school in Des Moines.

Luke opens the accordion door and motions her through.

She enters what must be the church's burial ground for old Sunday school supplies.

She spots two flannelboards, a rickety chalk board on rollers, a sewing machine, and stacks and stacks of boxes—mostly the kind used to ship fruit to market, all crammed, she supposes, with the wreckage of past programs, retreats, and Bible studies. In the far corner, a battered desk and two metal chairs could be part of the discarded junk, except that a fairly new phone sits on the desktop, the light on its pad blinking accusingly.

Luke sits, the metal chair shrieking under his weight. Mo takes the other chair, facing him. The phone rings. His hand engulfs the receiver.

"This is Luke . . . Hey, Marv . . . Yeah, yeah, yeah. I got the message . . . No. Not until 6:30 . . . No, it's at St. Vinnie's . . . Over on Fourth and Water . . . Yeah, that's right. You've been there . . . Yeah, yeah. Okay . . . Thanks. Yeah."

He cradles the phone. The light continues to blink. He turns toward her, smiling and nodding, as if expecting her to start the conversation.

"Maddie says you could use another helper," Mo says. When he continues to nod, she adds, "Put me in, coach. I'm ready to play."

"No hurry. Let's talk first."

The phone rings. Again he snatches up the receiver before it can sound a second ring. "This is Luke . . . Hey, Betty . . . Yeah. He just called."

Mo can hear the noise of preparations from the kitchen. Her metal chair creaks as she stands. She edges toward the door, but he motions with his free hand for her to sit.

"It's very hectic," she says when he hangs up.

"Par for the course. I did have to ask a gentleman to leave right before you got here."

"I think I saw him. Why did you–"

The phone again. Luke handles a short conversation with someone named Richard.

"I should get to work," Mo says. "It looks like there's plenty to do."

"Is that what you're here for? To work?"

"Well, yes. Isn't that the idea?"

Luke leans back, the chair groaning. "Let me tell you a story," he says.

The phone rings again.

"Yeah . . . Can I call you right back? . . . Yeah. Okay . . . No, I've got the number."

"So," he says as he hangs up. "Every summer I get an intern from the Christian College down in Goshen, Indiana. I can't remember how that got started, but it's been going on for years. A couple of years ago, they sent me a young lady who was all gung-ho to work. Couldn't get her to slow down long enough to breathe, let alone talk or eat. One day I asked her to come in here, and I sat her down, right where you're sitting."

Mo nods to show that's she's following the story.

"I told her this program isn't about working hard, and she got pretty mad. She even picked up a Bible and waved it at me." Rich, deep laughter seems to roll out of him.

"She quoted chapter and verse, about how The Good Book says a Christian is supposed to *feed* the *needy*. She said it just that way. '*Feed*' the '*needy*.'"

He stops, smiling expectantly at her. Not knowing what to say, she nods.

"So. I took her outside, where folks were lining up for the

meal. It was late in the month, and we had a pretty good line already. 'What about them?' I said. 'Are any of them Christians?'"

He laughs again, and Mo manages a smile.

"Well, she's *really* mad at me now!" Luke continues. "She kind of huffs at me, and she says, 'Well, maybe some of them.' And then we went back downstairs, and she went right back to running around like a one-armed paper-hanger."

He laughs again. "'Maybe some of them,'" he repeats.

"About how many will come to eat today?" she asks, slipping into interviewer mode.

"How many? Maybe 60. Maybe 100. You never know for sure."

"And you prepare the food here?"

"No, no. We don't have a license for that. Folks bring everything from home, and we heat it up here. Today's chili day."

"How do you know if you'll have enough?"

"Enough food?"

"Well, yes. And enough people to serve it."

"Oh, we always seem to manage."

The phone rings.

"Go talk to Elsie. She'll put you to work."

He grabs up the phone, and she escapes.

"This is Luke," she hears at her back. "Yeah, yeah, yeah." And then the rich laughter.

Elsie Lamb is putting bread into baskets on the large metal counter that bisects the right half of the kitchen. Maddie stands to her right, cutting sticks of butter in halves and putting the halves into small bowls.

"Luke sent me back here to get my assignment," Mo says.

"Did he now?"

"Monona! It is you!" Elsie Lamb exclaims, turning from her work to greet Mo.

Her former piano teacher seems to be part of the general time warp that has protected so much of the town from changing. Elsie Lamb is short and razor thin. She wears her gray hair pulled back off her narrow face. This is the same woman who instructed Mo to cup her hands and "pretend you're holding oranges" when she played the piano.

"Hi, Mrs. Lamb. It's so good to see you!"

"I think we can make it 'Elsie' now, don't you?"

"I'll try. How's Mr. Lamb?"

"Ezra? Cantankerous as ever. Worse when his back gets to paining him. He'll be along any minute."

A woman Elsie's age transfers mixed greens from a huge metal pan into serving bowls. Another woman carefully pours salad dressing from the bottle through a plastic funnel into a red, plastic squeeze container. Another fills clear plastic pitchers with milk. Two more are rinsing something out in a large double sink at the back. Heat and cooking odors emanate from an industrial oven behind the counter.

"Why don't you help Sophie and Mary Beth with the set-ups? We can always use a third hand there."

"Set-ups?"

"Napkins and silverware. You passed them on your way in. Come on. I'll introduce you to everybody, and we'll get you started."

All of the volunteers except for Maddie seem to be Elsie's age or older, and all are women except for the three men setting up the tables and chairs.

Sophie turns out to be from Norway, with a thick accent and a warm smile. Mary Beth is a tiny woman wearing a wide-brimmed hat and multi-colored scarf.

Mo is happily chatting with them, comfortable at last with a job to do, when Luke comes over and leans down next to her, his hands spread out on the table.

"Let me show you something," he says.

"Uh, oh," Sophie says, grinning. "He got you!"

"Am I doing it wrong?"

"No, no. Let me just show you a little secret."

He takes a napkin from the pile in the center of the table and gathers knife, fork, and spoon from the plastic holders. "What you do, see, is you set the silverware right about here, and then fold the flap of the napkin over the silverware before you roll it up." He demonstrates, handing her the finished set-up. "That way, the silverware can't fall out."

He picks up one she has just prepared, and knife, fork, and spoon clatter on the tile floor. "So," he says.

"Gotcha," she says. "Like a diaper."

"Yeah, yeah, yeah." He laughs as he moves on into the kitchen.

"Don't feel bad," Sophie says. "I've worked with that man for 17 years, and I've never gone a whole meal without getting busted at least once."

Mo, in fact, gets busted a second time, apparently for hurrying too much while putting set-ups and plastic cups on the tables.

"See, the thing is," Luke tells her, "we want folks to be able to relax and enjoy the meal. That's hard to do if people are running around like cats on a hot stove."

When preparations are complete, Luke gathers the helpers in a large circle at the back of the dining room.

"First, let's introduce ourselves. I'm Luke." He nods to his left.

"I'm Sophie."

"Pete."

"Elwood."

"I'm Monona," she says when it's her turn.

"I'm Maddie. Our mother insists we're related, but I don't see the resemblance."

They finish up the circle with John and Sarah, Martha, Mary Beth, and Caroline. They hold hands around the circle, heads bowed, eyes closed.

"Heavenly Father," Luke says, "we thank you for bringing us together this day. We pray for all who are sick, and especially for Char, who has her eye operation today, and for Mike, who's in hospice. We pray for the homeless, for those without families as the holidays approach, for all those who lack the necessities of life. We ask you to bless all who share a meal here this day. And we ask it in Jesus' name."

"Amen," Mo choruses with the rest.

"Okay. Jobs," Luke says. "Elsie, you'll quarterback the kitchen, right?"

"Aye, aye."

"Dishing up? Sophie? You want to start out in the kitchen, and Mary Beth, you can spell her after you've eaten?"

Luke gets volunteers for "reset" and finally for "serving."

"I'll tote chili," Maddie says.

"Me, too," Mo says.

"Good. Maddie and Sara, you can work first shift, and Mo, you eat first and then take over for one of them."

"Oh, that's okay," Mo says. "I don't need to eat."

"Yeah, yeah, yeah. Go sit down. Let your sister wait on you."

Reluctantly, Mo goes to the far table, which is set for eight diners, where Pete already sits, hands folded in front of him on the table.

"Hi," Mo says, taking the seat next to him.

He nods and smiles but says nothing.

The servers take their stations. Luke disappears up the side steps. Maddie approaches, carrying a tray with four bowls of steaming chili. Elwood is right behind her with another tray, and he slides a bowl of chili onto the plate in front of Mo.

"Enjoy," he says. "What's up, Pete?"

Pete nods, eyes on his chili.

Luke appears at the foot of the stairs, followed by a string of people, whom he seats at the open spaces at the three tables until every space is taken. A line of people remains along the far wall, waiting patiently for a turn to eat.

"Chili!" a small man across the table from her exclaims. "*Que lastima!*"

"*Comida del puerco,*" the man next to him says.

The man to his left laughs, a harsh cackle, his open mouth displaying large gaps between his yellowing teeth. A shaggy mustache covers his upper lip.

His long, black hair is a wild tangle. He looks, Mo decides, like a demented jack-o-lantern.

"It's better than nada, amigos," he tells them. He shovels chili into his mouth, his hand gripping the spoon like a cudgel.

The first man eyes Mo from across the table.

"I take it you don't like chili," she says to him.

The man's eyebrow arches slightly. "*Habla Espanol!*"

"*Un poco, solemente,*" Mo assures him.

"Ah. *Un poco.* Like Eddie here says, is better than nada, huh? Pass the pimiento, por favor."

Mo passes both salt and pepper shakers across the table.

"*Como se llama?*" she tries, feeling as self-conscious as when she was stumbling through verb conjugations in Señor Reyes's high school class.

"*Me llamo* Juan," he says, and Mo now sees that he is a good bit older than she had, at first, thought. "*Et usted?*"

"*Me llamo* Mo," she says, then quickly adds "*Por* Monona. Monona Quinn."

"*Mucho gusto, Señora* Mo."

"*Mucho gusto, Señor* Juan."

The two men next to him break into raucous laughter. Juan nudges his companion, who nudges him back, still giggling.

"Forgive my noisy friend," he says to Mo. "Señora Quinn, this is mi amigo, Eddie Rodriquez. Eddie, la Señora Quinn." He says Quinn like "queen."

"*Con mucho gusto!*" Eddie says.

"I'm Ross," the man to his left says. "Ross Grimsled." Again the cackling laugh, the horrid teeth.

The other five at the table have busied themselves passing salad and bread, pouring milk or water, and making various preparations to their chili. They don't seem to want to talk. But Ross Grimsled appears willing to do the talking for everyone.

"Old Luke," he says, to no one in particular, "he sure gave old Ryno the bum's rush, didn't he?"

The two Mexican Americans nod. Eddie grins. The others at the table ignore Ross, and he keeps talking.

"Whoo-whee. Out the door you go! Old Lukie. He don't take nothin' off nobody." Grimsled crams most of a slice of heavily buttered bread into his mouth and continues to talk. "Old Blin' Ryne, he don't know what hit him."

"Oh, he knows, all right," Juan says.

Mo drags her eyes from Ross Grimsled, trying not to think of carved pumpkins.

"They are talking about the man we call 'Blind Ryne,'" Juan tells her.

"If you took off his glasses, he would walk right into a tree!"

"Or try to strike up a conversation with it," Grimsled says, unleashing his cackle.

"He is a great man," Eddie says gravely. "He marched with Chavez."

"Cesar Chavez," Juan explains. "He founded Huelga."

"The California farm workers," Mo says.

"Ah! You know of him!"

"Yes, I—"

"I know this," Eddie says, "because I was *there*." He sits up straighter in his chair. "I, too, marched with Chavez."

"Yeah, and you helped Moses carry the stone tablets down off that mountain, didn't you, Señor?" Grimsled says.

Eddie looks away. Grimsled crams another slice of bread into his mouth.

Mo eats her chili, which has chunks of tomato, onion, and mushroom. When she has finished, she stacks her plate and cup, as she has seen others do, and stands. "It's been very nice eating with you," she says. "I have to go work now."

"*Mucho gusto*, Señora Mo," Juan says.

Eddie stands. "*Mucho gusto*, Señora," he says, bowing from the waist.

"Hey!" Ross Grimsley's harsh interjection freezes her.

"Yes?"

"Nice talking with you," he says, and unleashes another cackling laugh.

She hurries to the kitchen window, where Maddie and Sara stand, trays in hand, waiting for the clean-up crew to finish resetting one of the tables.

"Okay. I'm ready to work."

"You want to eat next, Sara?" Maddie says.

"You go ahead."

"Good. I'm hungry."

Mo watches her sister take her place at the end of the line. Standing at the front of that line, Luke raises his index finger and makes circles with it.

"Full table," Sara says to Mary Beth behind the counter, and the tiny woman begins ladling up bowls of steaming chili from the large metal pot in front of her.

Mo manages to get four bowls of chili to the table and onto plates without mishap. As she carries her tray back to the window, she notices someone at another table has left a half-full bowl of chili and several bread crusts. She scoops them up onto her tray and continues toward the back.

"Uh, oh. Look out," Sara mutters. "Here comes trouble."

Luke bears down on her as she returns to the kitchen window. "Whoa, whoa, whoa," he says, rubbing his hands on his apron. "Don't be doing that."

"What?"

"Don't be cleaning up tables. That's not your job."

"Yes, but—"

"Here's the thing. The people who serve the chili have clean hands. The folks who clean up the tables have dirty hands. You don't want dirty hands touching the chili. You know? You get your thumb in there, and somebody sees it, and says 'I'm not going to eat that!'" He laughs, expectant eyes on her.

"I understand."

"Good, good."

"You got it twice!" Sara says, chuckling, when Mo returns from washing her hands at the back sink.

"Three times. You missed one. He told me to slow down."

Sara laughs. "Don't worry," she says. "You're a long way from breaking any records."

Maddie returns, releasing Sara to eat lunch. The rest of the shift goes quickly, a steady stream of folks replacing the diners as they finish their meals.

"Thank you very much," one of them says to Mo as she circles one of the tables, offering cookies from a tray. "It was a very fine meal."

"Thank you for coming."

"Where do all these people come from?" Mo asks her sister when the lunch hour has ended. They are standing side by side at the counter, Mo pouring milk from pitchers back into bottles, and Maddie putting leftover butter into a plastic container. "It seems as if we fed half the town."

"Some come from a long ways off," Maddie says.

"I had no idea there would be so many."

"Everybody talks about the urban poor, but there's an awful lot of poverty out here on the farm. Luke's been running this program for over 20 years."

"Really? He doesn't look old enough."

"How old do you think he is?"

"I don't know. Forty, maybe. I guess he's older than he looks, huh?"

"He's in his middle fifties."

"You're kidding. He can't be."

"He is, though. He played football for Summerfeld when we won State."

"I don't even remember that."

"Of course you don't. It was before we were born."

"I guess everybody will be at the game tonight, huh?"

"Oh, the joint will be jumping," Maddie assures her.

"Do you think Aidan will change his mind and come with us?"

She sees the sudden pain on her sister's face and wishes she hadn't asked.

"No," Maddie says simply. "I'm sure he won't. I don't know what's going on inside him. He's certainly angry, and scared—and has a right to be. But there's something else, something he's not telling me. Something he's not telling anybody. I'm as sure of that as I am about anything on this earth.

"I just keep hoping maybe he'll tell you."

7

Lined up for their mother's inspection, Matt, Mark, and Chance Logan look like the same red-haired, freckled boy in three different sizes.

Wrecker twines among them, hoping to come along but knowing better.

"If we win this one and the one next week, it's off to Waterloo, boys!" Everett Logan tells his three sons.

"Now, you boys be on your best behavior," warns Emily Logan, 'Emmy' to her husband and friends. She tries to pat down Mark's cowlick, but he fends her off, grumbling, "Aw, Mom!"

"It's a football game, Emmy," Everett tells her. "Not a dance."

"I don't want them behaving like barbarians. You, either."

"Why don't you come along? You can keep us in line."

"Yeah, come on, Mom!" Chance pleads.

"Mrs. Quinn and I have plenty needs doing here. I'll leave it to you to root the boys on to State."

"You sure you ladies don't want to hop into the back of the truck?" Everett says to Mo, with a wink to Maddie.

"Don't you dare!" Emily says. "He hasn't cleaned that thing out since he took Pygmalion over to the Sprecher's to stud."

"Pygmalion," Chance says happily. "P-U!"

"We'll meet you there, thanks just the same," Maddie says.

"Suit yourselves," says Everett. "Come on, boys. We want to get good seats."

"Can Danny ride with us?" Chance asks Maddie.

"Can I, Mom?"

"If it's okay with Mr. Logan."

"Can I, Mr. Logan?"

Everett smiles at him. "Hop in," he says.

"Oh, boy!" Danny turns to Mo. "Is that okay, Aunt Monona?"

"Sure."

"I got shotgun," Chance says, racing around the pickup to the passenger side door. Danny piles in ahead of him, and Chance slams the door. Matt hoists himself up on the side of the truck bed and swings his legs over, landing on his feet. Mark tries to match his brother's feat but winds up rolling over the side and landing in a heap.

"Way to go, doofus," Matt laughs at the same time as his mother says, "You boys be careful! And don't stand up while the truck is moving! You hear me?"

"We hear you, Ma," Matt assures her. "And don't worry. I'll hang onto doofus, here, so he doesn't fall out."

Mark gets to his feet and slugs his big brother on the arm. He receives a return slug. Their father's stern, "That'll do, gentlemen!" quells the potential scuffle.

"Danny's such a great kid," Mo says as she climbs in on the passenger side of the Durning family pickup.

"He has his moments, believe me." Maddie turns the ignition key, and the engine flares to life. "He's so excited that you're coming to his talent show."

"Wouldn't miss it."

The sun has already set, the soft after-light spread out across the broad western horizon, as Mo and Maddie head out onto Durning-Quinn Road behind the Logan's pickup. Mark and Matt sit with their backs to the cab, identical feed caps pulled low over their eyes, their knees up. They bounce and sway with the bumps and curves in the road.

"Danny doesn't show it, but this mess with Aidan has really thrown him," Maddie admits as she slows for an erosion gully in the road.

"I can imagine."

"Danny has always looked up to Aidan, but since Kenny left, he's really relied on his big brother. Aidan can do no wrong in his eyes. I don't think he understands how his hero could have gotten mixed up with drugs."

The road soon fills with cars and pickups, many flying Summerfeld blue and gold from their radio antennae. At the four-way stop at Lowrey's Corners, a long line of traffic stretches out in both directions. The horn honking is friendly, and many roll down their windows to wave and shout.

"Looks like everybody and his brother's coming," Maddie says.

And indeed, the stands are already filling rapidly as Maddie noses the pickup onto the large, open field behind the high school and parks in the place indicated by a man in an orange hunting vest.

"What kept you?" Everett greets them as they approach the opening in the fence, where smiling volunteers are tearing tickets and hawking game programs.

"I brake for pigs and cows," Maddie says, laughing. "You just fly right over them."

They find seats high up on the home-team side on about the 25-yard line.

The wooden bench is hard, the legroom scarce, the aisle a long way away—but the spirit of the crowd is irresistible. Leggy cheerleaders, pompoms shedding blue and gold, prance in front of the stands while the band assembles on the sideline and the two teams run through their warm-up drills on opposite ends of the field. Pickup trucks line both end zones, their lights casting long shadows from the goal posts. The home team wears white pants and jerseys with navy blue numerals outlined in gold. On each helmet, the silhouette of a man on a rearing horse makes it clear that the team is the mighty Cowboys.

"Hey, Clabe!" Everett hollers from his seat between Mark on his left and Chance on his right. A thin, weathered man in baggy overalls pauses in the aisle to tip up his seed cap and squint to see who hailed him. He hunches over, his bony shoulders up around his ears. Pieces of painted wood peek from his breast pocket, and a hammer hangs from a loop at his waist.

"Hey, there, Ev!" he shouts back.

"What's the line?"

"Cowboys and three!"

"Think they'll cover?"

"My money says they will." The man tugs his cap low over his eyes and continues his ascent.

"Clabe Profitt," Everett tells Mo, talking across Chance and Danny. "He's got the hardware store in town. He and his brother, Esau, but Esau don't help run it no more."

"It's a neat store, Auntie Mo," Danny says. "They've got little tractors."

"He's got quite a display of farm toys," Maddie adds. "It's not as big an attraction as the Cowboy Museum, of course, but it's something to see."

"You wanna, Aunt Mo? You wanna see it tomorrow?"

"That's the talent show, honey," Maddie reminds him.

"Oh, yeah!"

The public address announcer runs through the starting lineups, the players for the visiting Rock River Rangers drawing cheers from the opposite side of the field, the Cowboy starters receiving much louder shouts and whistles from the home side.

The crowd stands as the drummers lay out a solemn roll, and the ROTC unit presents the colors at midfield. Reigning Miss Falkner County, Shelley Stricker, flawlessly renders the National Anthem.

"That's the way to sing it!" Everett shouts.

They remain standing as the Rangers kick off to the Cowboys' number 26, Ronnie Waddell, who takes the ball on the goal line and returns it out to the 22-yard line.

The two teams push each other back and forth for several exchanges of the ball, neither offense advancing the ball across midfield.

"Why don't they do something, Daddy?" Chance laments after the Cowboys punt for the third time.

"They're just feeling each other out," his father tells him, "like a couple of prize fighters in the early rounds. Don't you worry. They'll get going."

"Come on, Cowboys!" Maddie yells.

"They miss Aidan out there," Mo tells her.

On their first series of the second quarter, the Cowboys mount a drive, Rick Sherman connecting on three crisp third-down passes in a row to James Breckner, "his favorite target,"

Everett tells them. But the drive stalls when Sherman gets sacked behind the line of scrimmage, trying to find an open receiver.

"Come on, dog!" a man hollers loudly enough to be heard from his front row seat on the 50-yard line, directly behind the Cowboys' bench. "Get your ass in gear!"

"Yeah," Chance says, giggling. "Get your ass in gear."

"That's enough of that!" his father tells him.

"But that man said it."

"That don't make it okay for you to say it, son."

"Who is he?" Mo asks Maddie. "He's been riding our poor quarterback all game."

"That's Russell Sherman, Rick's father."

"You're kidding."

"He's always like that. Goes to every practice and every game, home and away. No matter how well Rick plays, it's never good enough for his father."

"That's terrible!"

"His father's also his agent. He's handling all the college recruiters, and he's already had conversations with pro scouts, or so they say."

"Rick's still just a kid!"

"A million dollar kid. Everybody expects him to be a big star. His father plans to have him play two years at State and then transfer to USC."

The Rangers march steadily down the field, keeping the ball on the ground, their big fullback, Eddie Tyler, churning up yardage with plunges into the center of the line. The Cowboys stiffen with their backs to their own goal line when Sherman, playing safety on defense, flicks a third-down pass away from the intended receiver in the end zone. Rock River tries a field goal, but the wobbly kick hits the crossbar and bounces away.

"Now it's our turn, boys!" Everett yells.

But on the Cowboys' next series, Sherman fades to pass on third down and long and gets blindsided just as he steps up to throw. The ball squirts free, and a Ranger defender scoops it up and sprints into the end zone for the game's first score. The kick for the extra point clears the uprights, but only just.

"7-0!" Chance wails. "We're losing!"

"Don't worry, son," his father says. "There's a lot of football left. We ain't licked yet.

"Makes it tougher to cover the spread, though," he admits, directing the comment to Maddie and Mo.

"Do people bet a lot on high school football?" Mo asks him.

Everett snorts. "You kiddin'? There'll be more action on this game in Iowa than on the Super Bowl."

"Really?"

"Oh, yeah. Rumor has it that Rindeknect runs the biggest bookie ring in the state from right here in Summerfeld."

"Rindeknect?"

"'Blind Ryne,' they call him. "Sheriff 's had his eye on that guy for months, but so far, he hasn't been able to pin anything on him."

Mo turns to her sister. "Wasn't that the name of the man who got thrown out at lunch today?" she asks.

Maddie shrugs. "I didn't hear about that."

The crowd leaps to its feet and explodes in cheers. Mo jumps up but still can't see past the man in front of her.

"Thatta baby!" Everett crows, hopping up on the bench and pumping his fist in the air. "Now we're playing some football!"

Ronnie Waddell has returned a short Ranger kickoff all the way back across the 50-yard line and into enemy territory. His sweep around left end nets eight more yards, and on the next play Sherman hits Breckner on a slant pattern over the middle, the flanker running the ball to the Ranger 16 before being forced out of bounds.

"We're gonna get a touchdown, Auntie Mo!" Danny squeals, hugging her.

"Don't count your chickens, son," Everett tells him. "We got it to get yet. And there's only time for one more play, two at the most, before halftime."

Sherman calls a timeout and trots over to the sidelines to confer with Coach Harley Hunt.

Maddie has climbed onto the bleacher seat and steadies herself with a hand on her sister's shoulder. "Go! Go! Go!" she screams, and Mo finds herself screaming along.

Even above the steady din of the crowd, they can hear the hoarse, raspy voice of Russell Sherman. "Stick it to 'em, dog! Don't let 'em get back up!"

"All right. Here we go," Everett says as the Cowboys break their huddle.

Maddie grips Mo's shoulder so tightly it hurts.

The quarterback surveys the defense as he walks slowly to the line of scrimmage. He slaps the center on the rear and steps back.

"He's gonna take it off the shotgun," Everett tells them.

As the crowd stills, the young man's voice carries clearly into the stands. "Red 19! V-54. Hut-hut, hut."

The snap from center sails over Sherman's head and bounds upfield. With Ranger defenders charging after him, Sherman turns, sprints back, scoops up the ball on the run, and spins back toward the goal. He eludes one would-be tackler, straight-arms another, picks up a block, and heads toward the far sidelines as the gun sounds. A Ranger dives and misses him, and Sherman literally hurdles another attempted tackle, with a swarm of Rangers closing in on him.

With nowhere to go, he lowers his head and is buried in red-shirted Rangers at the 15-yard line.

"Aw, nerts!" Chance says. "Now we're going to lose."

His father's attention is riveted on the field, where Rick Sherman has yet to get up. "Ohmagosh," Everett murmurs. "Ohmagosh."

"Is he hurt, Dad?" Chance says.

"No, birdbrain," Mark says. "He's taking a nap."

"Hush, now," Everett warns.

The crowd is silent as Coach Hunt and a man in a business suit bend over the young star—but it lets out a collective sigh before bursting into cheers as Sherman gets up. The two men flank him, their hands seeming to offer only token support on each arm as he walks off the field.

"He went on his own steam," Everett says. "That's good. That's real good."

"We'd lose without him, wouldn't we, Dad?" Chance asks.

"We're losing *with* him, stupid," Mark says.

"That's enough, son!" Everett says.

The Cowboy cheerleaders form a six-person pyramid in front of the bleachers. The young lady at the top stands, arms outstretched, head thrown back, and executes a back flip into the waiting arms of a male cheerleader.

Mo goes with Danny and Chance to get hotdogs and sodas at the concession stand run by the PTO behind the bleachers. The line is long, and by the time they get back, the teams are already back on the field for the start of the third quarter.

"Do you think we'll win, Aunt Monona?" Danny asks anxiously.

"Sure we'll win!" Chance insists. "Rick'll come through."

But the Rangers score on another Cowboy mistake. This time a tipped pass falls into the hands of a Ranger defensive back, who runs it in for the touchdown and a 14-0 lead.

With the crowd pleading for the Cowboys to come to life, Sherman leads his troops downfield on a long touchdown march to put Summerfeld on the board. The defense stiffens, and Sherman strikes again early in the fourth quarter on a beautiful 67-yard catch and run by Breckner. After the extra point is again successful, the Cowboys have tied the game, 14-14.

"Come on!" Danny wails, bouncing up and down on the bleachers. "You can do it!"

"I think we just might!" Everett allows. "I think we just might!"

The ensuing kickoff tumbles end over end into the arms of the charging Ranger at the 27-yard line and he roars straight up field, cuts over to the far sideline, and carries the ball all the way into the Cowboy end zone.

The crowd, so boisterous just seconds before, sits in disbelieving silence.

A moment later, they cheer as the Rangers try for the extra point barely makes it over the line of scrimmage and falls harmlessly in the end zone.

"We're still alive!" Everett says, reaching out to rumple Matt's hair.

With time running out and the game on the line, Rick Sherman takes over. Deftly mixing sweeps and plunges into the center of the line with short possession passes, he moves his team into Ranger territory. A penalty for holding sets them back, but on third down and long, Sherman hits Breckner on a perfectly timed sideline pass, and Breckner steps out of bounds at the Ranger 27, one yard beyond the first-down marker.

"A field goal doesn't help us," Everett reminds them. "We gotta go for the TD."

With less than two minutes left, a championship, and the chance to go to the regional playoffs at stake, Mo is as caught up in the drama as any other in the crowd.

A slant pass fails when the ball and a defender hit Breckner at the same time.

"Isn't that pass interference, Dad?" Mark asks, and the booing crowd seems to agree.

"Clean hit, son," Everett says. "Or at least too close to call. You don't want the refs deciding the game now."

"Come on!" Maddie murmurs, fingers crossed. "Come on!"

Sherman fades as if to pass and hands the ball off on a draw play to the fullback, but big Frank Conrad finds the going tough in the middle of the line, advancing the ball only two hard yards. Third and eight, with the clock running.

"What kind of a bonehead call was that?" Matt fumes.

"Watch, now," Everett tells him. "See how he's got the defensive backs cheating in toward the line of scrimmage. You watch now."

Sherman fakes a handoff to Waddell and rolls out to his right.

"Play action!" Everett says, poking Chance on the arm. "Watch this!"

Streaking straight down the right sidelines, Breckner has managed to get a step behind the defensive back, but the safety is coming over quickly to help out. As two linebackers close in on him, Sherman sprints toward the sidelines and launches a perfect spiral downfield. The ball arches just over the outstretched fingertips of a defender and into Breckner's hands as he crosses the goal line.

The gun sounds.

The crowd roars.

"It's a tie!" Danny shouts. "It's a tie!"

"No, no," Everett says. "We still get to kick the extra point. That's the rule."

"What if they block it?" Chance asks.

"You gotta think positive, son."

The Rangers's coach tries to call a timeout, and the refs confer to decide if it's legal to call a timeout when there's no time left.

"What are they doing?" Chance asks, frowning.

"They're icing the kicker," Matt tells his brother. "Giving him time to think about the kick and get real nervous."

"We just have to win, Auntie Mo. We just have to!" Danny says.

"Both teams are trying their hardest," Mo tells him. "Somebody has to lose."

"I want *them* to lose!"

"So do I!" Maddie says.

The refs decide the Rangers can't have a timeout and order the teams back onto the field. The Cowboys line up in kick formation, with Breckner to receive the snap from center for Sherman to attempt the kick. The Rangers send 10 men up to the line of scrimmage, ready for an all-out charge, while the eleventh jumps up and down behind the line, waving his arms and, no doubt, screaming, although he can't be heard over the crowd.

"Get a good snap," Everett coaxes.

"Come on come on come on come on," Maddie murmurs, eyes shut.

Danny squeezes Mo's hand so tightly, she fears she may never regain sensation in the fingers.

The snap. The placement. The kick.

Perfect.

Cowboys 21, Rangers 20.

The Cowboys go to the divisional playoffs. The Rangers go home.

The home crowd stays to cheer its team and sing the Summerfeld alma mater, "Blue and gold, all hail to thee. Summer-feld." The bleachers empty slowly. Drivers honk and passengers wave and shout out the open windows as the Summerfeld caravan wends its way home.

"That was the best game in the history of the world!" Danny says from his perch between Maddie and Mo on the bench seat of the Durning pickup. "I knew we'd win! I just knew it!"

"I don't understand how they can win but still lose," Maddie says, braking sharply as the traffic in front of her slows suddenly.

"We didn't lose! We won!" Danny insists.

"I know, honey. But Mr. Logan was talking about how they didn't cover."

"The point spread," Mo says.

"What's a point spread, Aunt Mo?"

She glances at her sister, who shrugs.

"People bet on who will win the game," Mo begins.

"I know that," Danny says.

"If most folks think Summerfeld will win, not very many people will bet against them," Mo explains. "So you have to give the other side points."

"To make it even?" Danny asks.

"To make it interesting, anyway," Mo says.

"Like a handicap in golf," Maddie says.

"So, if you take Summerfeld and three points, Summerfeld not only has to win, but they have to win by at least four points for you to collect your bet."

"What if they win by three points?" Danny asks.

"Then it's a push. A tie. Neither side wins."

"So people who bet on Summerfeld still lost, even though we won?"

"Yes."

"That's stupid. We won."

"That's right!" his mother agrees. "Rock River can have its points."

"I agree that it's stupid," Mo says. "And also probably very lucrative for local bookies. Everett says there was a lot of money riding on the game."

"What's a 'bookie'?" Danny asks.

"Oh, Lord," Maddie says. "Let's see you explain that one."

"I'm not sure I can," Mo says, laughing. "Wait a minute. Maybe I can. You know about the twelve disciples, right?"

"Sure."

"And you remember that one of them, Judas, 'held the common purse'?"

"Judas betrayed Jesus."

"That's right. He also took money out of the purse for himself."

"Was he a *bookie*?"

Maddie snorts. "Keep digging," she says to Mo. "You've just about buried yourself."

"Not exactly," Mo says, ignoring her sister. "The bookie holds the purse, all the money that gets bet. If lots of people lose their bets, the bookie gets to keep lots of money."

"What if the people all win their bets?"

"Then the bookie's in a heap of trouble."

"Ev says the bookie hardly ever loses," Maddie tells her sister. "He gets some kind of percentage on every bet. Like a commission."

"I'll bet they charge hefty interest rates on unpaid bets, too."

Traffic has thinned, but folks still honk and wave as they pass one another. Danny's head sags onto Mo's shoulder, and his regular breathing tells her that he has finally run out of energy and fallen asleep. She rides in silence, glancing over at her sister, seeing the worry lines on her face; seeing, too, the determination that has carried her through so much and will have to carry her through so much more. Mo's heart fills with love and admiration for her twin, who grew up at her side. "Two perfect reflections of God's love," their mother used to say. "And," she always added, "proof of His sense of humor."

Their mother is asleep, the house dark, when they get home. Mo helps Danny upstairs and into bed, while Maddie walks up the road to the Quinn farmhouse to check with Everett on his work plans for the next day.

When Maddie comes back, the sisters sit together in the family room, sipping cocoa and looking out over fields of dried corn stalks.

"That's about all the excitement I can handle for one day," Mo says. "Life on the farm is too wild for me!"

"Don't forget the talent show tomorrow."

"No way I'd forget that."

"I hope Danny does well. He's been practicing and practicing."

"He'll be fine. Wait until you hear his patter."

"I see so much of Kenny in him. The boundless energy and enthusiasm, especially. The stubbornness and temper, too. Speaking of Kenny, I'd better check the phone messages." Maddie stands with a tired groan. "He's not due to call until tomorrow night, but I always check anyway."

From the other room, Mo hears Kenny's tinny recorded voice on the answering machine, a beep, and then a higher, melodious voice, speaking rapidly, another beep. Maddie appears in the doorway.

"Eileen's coming!" she says.

For a moment, Mo thinks she means their mother, sleeping soundly in the first-floor den that Kenny converted into a bedroom for her. "Little Eileen!" she says, understanding.

"Little Eileen," Maddie confirms, smiling. "Our college girl."

"That's wonderful! I'm so glad I'll get to see her. Is she on break already?"

"No." Maddie sits in the rocker next to Mo. "She wasn't going to come home until Thanksgiving. But she said she wants to see her Auntie Mo."

They leave the rest unsaid. She's no doubt coming now out of concern for her twin brother and for her mother.

Upstairs in Aidan's room, Mo checks her own phone messages on her cell and sees that she has none. She has three emails from Vi, newspaper stuff, none of it an emergency; she decides to handle it in the morning.

No message from Doug, phone or email.

She considers calling, decides it's too late, starts an email and then, with a surge of anger and resentment, deletes it unsent.

She logs off, gets ready for bed, and crawls in under the covers with the new John Dunning "Bookman" mystery, but finds herself too tired and sad to read. She clicks off the light, letting the book slide onto the bed next to her. Darkness and quiet fill the little room. The house sighs. The moon shows faintly outside the south side window, casting a pale glow on the room.

She wakes with a start. In the darkness, a harsh whirring noise offends the silence. The bathroom fan, she tells herself. That thing is loud!

But who's in the bathroom?

No need to be alarmed, she tells herself. A prowler would hardly come upstairs and use the facility. It's probably just Danny. Or Aiden—there's no plumbing in the barn, and this is his bathroom, after all.

She gets up, puts on her bathrobe, clicks on the light, and sits on the bed, waiting. The whirring stops abruptly. The bathroom door scrapes the jam as it opens. Aidan's face appears at the doorway.

"Sorry, Aunt Mo. I didn't mean to wake you."

"That's all right."

"I hear we won tonight."

"Just barely. They missed you."

"Ha!" It's more bark than laugh, no happiness in it.

"Thanks for giving me your room. It's nice."

"Mom says it's a pig sty. I wasn't using it anyway."

"Yeah. I hear you're out in the barn loft now."

"Yep. A regular penthouse."

"Come in and sit for a minute with your favorite Auntie."

"You always said that." He crosses the room and straddles the desk chair. "Ever since I was little."

"I figured if I said it often enough, you'd believe it."

"I don't know of anybody else who has an aunt who solves murders."

"My reputation is exaggerated, believe me."

"Do you miss it? Writing for the *Trib* and all?"

The question gives her pause. "Yeah," she admits. "Sometimes."

"I'll bet it was a real rush."

"Pure panic at deadline."

He nods. They fall silent.

"Listen," he says.

"What?"

"Coyote. Way off. Everett says he's gonna shoot it, but I don't think the coyote will let him get close enough. God, that's a lonesome sound."

Mo nods, her eyes on her nephew. He has filled out, his six-foot-plus frame now solid with muscle. His face seems harder, older; no longer the happy, guileless little boy's face.

"Your sister called. She's coming home."

"Oh, yeah? Awesome."

"You two were so close growing up. Was it hard, her going off to college a year ahead of you?"

He looks away. "She was into her own thing anyway."

"It must be rough with your dad gone."

"It's real hard on Mom. And then I go and screw up like this."

"You want to talk about it?"

He shakes his head, a single, quick movement. He stands, towering over her. He digs a hand into the pocket of his denims, pulls out a handful of change, sorts through, finds the coin he wants, and hands it to her.

"Dad gave it to me before he left. For luck."

One side of the coin depicts a woman carrying a baby in a blanket on her back, her face turned outward. Above her is the word LIBERTY, and behind her, where her braid goes behind the baby's head, the words IN GOD WE TRUST. On the flip side, an eagle, wings spread, soars toward the words E PLUREBUS UNUM. UNITED STATES OF AMERICA arches over the top of the eagle, with ONE DOLLAR below.

"A Sacachewea dollar," she says. "You hardly ever see these."

"Dad keeps one with him all the time, too."

Mo hands the coin back, and Aidan puts it in his pocket.

She stands. "Got a hug for your favorite auntie?"

He grins. "Oh, I guess so," he says.

He hugs her awkwardly, his body rigid, the muscles of his arms hard.

"Night, Auntie Mo."

"Good night, Scooter."

He grins again, even laughs. "You haven't called me that in a long time," he says.

"You'll always be my little putt-putt scooter."

He lingers at the door. "Thanks for coming," he says.

"Of course. You say a prayer for your dad."

"I will."

And then he's gone.

She hears him thud down the stairs and across the family room, hears the door open and shut softly behind him. From the window, she sees him cross the yard and slip through the narrow gap in the barn door. She takes off her bathrobe, crawls back under the covers, and snaps off the lamp by the bed. The grandfather clock strikes the hour downstairs. Two AM. She's still awake when it strikes three.

Mo had forgotten the magic of morning on the farm, and especially the smells of growing things, and of the land getting ready for its long winter dormancy.

Birds sing, water riffles gently, a breeze flutters the last leaves clinging obstinently to the oaks and birches. In the eastern sky, gentle yellows spread to coat the low clouds hugging the horizon.

Above all, she savors the incredible freshness of the air, like sweet, clear water, and the joy of her body in motion, the dirt road under her feet, her lungs laboring just slightly. She thinks of Doug and his pre-dawn jog.

"Compulsive," she has called it. Maybe there's something more to it after all.

She realizes how much she has missed this farm, this land, this sense of belonging, of rightness, of being where she's supposed to be, doing what she's supposed to be doing.

Wrecker joins her for the greater part of her walk, out past the Quinn farm and the family cemetery and along Summerfeld Creek and the great woods, which had seemed endless when she and Maddie explored them together as children.

She tries a few of Maddie's commands on her happy, willing

trail companion, and he seems content to heel at her left side until she releases him with a cheerful, "Okay!" as she has heard Maddie do. She's glad for his company and misses him when he turns in at his farm on her way back. She has to fight the urge to turn up that driveway herself; for all of her growing-up years, that was home.

In a sense, it will always be home.

Her thoughts merge into a prayer of praise and thanksgiving. Who, in the face of such glorious creation, could doubt the existence of a loving Creator?

Doug, for one. She prays for him, for his safety and well-being and for faith to find him; for her mother, losing her hold on what they know of reality; for Kenny, in harm's way in Iraq, for Maddie and Aidan and Eileen. She holds up each of her loved ones in turn for God's blessing and grace.

As she turns in at the Durning farm, she notes that the pickup truck is gone and remembers that Maddie needed to leave early to pick up Eileen at the airport in the city. She had planned to go along. No regrets, she tells herself. You have chosen the greater portion.

She hears the piano playing from well down the driveway, the flowing power of "Fur Elise," another strong connection to childhood.

Her mother hears the door open behind her and turns, embarrassed, as if caught in mischief.

"Please don't stop. It sounds wonderful."

"Oh." Her thin, veiny hand waves at the air. "I just do it to keep my fingers limber."

"Does it hurt? To play?"

"Sometimes more than others. Sit down. Do you remember our song?"

Mo slides in next to her mother on the bench. Her left hand searches out the keys, F for the pinky, A for the middle finger, C for the pointer. She begins playing the chord in sets of four and three, emphasizing the first chord of each set.

"Now your boop-de-do's."

Mo's right hand crosses over to play C-C-D-E in quick succession before each chord set. Her mother begins to play, her right hand seeming to dance on the keys as she picks out the bouncy melody. By the time they finish, Mo is laughing with pure joy. She puts her arm around her mother's shoulder and squeezes.

"You played that for our class at school," she says, the memory filling her with wonder. "We danced to it."

"That's right."

"What's the name of that song?"

"I have no idea. I don't know if I ever knew. I might have made it up."

"None of the boys wanted to dance."

"Except Jerry Dolan. He had a huge crush on you."

"He did not."

"He most certainly did."

"If anything, he had a thing for Maddie."

"No, ma'am. It was you he gave the valentine to, a big, red heart with lacey edges."

"He gave everyone a valentine."

"Just those little ones that come nine to a page and when you press them out, they still have the little knobby edges on them."

"Really?"

"Listen, kiddo. I'm at the stage where I can't remember what I had for breakfast, but I remember your second grade class, yours and Maddie's, like it was yesterday."

"What did you have for breakfast?"

Her mother frowns. "I can't remember." She laughs. "I don't think I've eaten yet."

"Play something else. Please."

"Oh."

But she begins to play a progression of notes with her left hand, all on black keys. Mo laughs and claps her hands.

"The opening riff of 'What I say?'! That's wonderful!"

They sit for a moment, smiling into each other's eyes.

"I haven't had breakfast either," Mo says, getting up. "And I'm hungry!"

"I can make you eggs and sausage."

"Don't you dare. I saw some low-fat granola in the cupboard."

Mo gets up, and her mother follows her into the kitchen. Her mother settles in at the kitchen table and lets her daughter pour her a cup of coffee.

"Can I get you something, Mom?"

"I guess I could eat a couple of pieces of toast."

"Is that all you want?"

"That's plenty. Thank you, dear."

Mo puts two slices of wheat bread in the toaster and gets herself a bowl of cereal.

"You don't actually eat that stuff, do you? It looks like you ought to pour it into the trough and let the cows have at it."

"You'd go broke fast," Mo says, slicing a banana on her cereal and going to the refrigerator for milk. "This stuff is expensive!"

"You go broke milking cows anyway. You might as well do it fast."

By the time the pickup clatters up the gravel driveway and slams to a stop by the house three hours later, Mo and her

mother have Eileen's favorite dinner—roast beef, mashed potatoes, peas and carrots, and scratch biscuits—almost ready, with
an apple pie cooling on the counter.

"Guess who's here!" Danny shouts as he pounds across the
lawn to where his Aunt Mo and Grammy Quinn stand on the
porch.

"Santa Claus," Grammy says.

"No!" Danny thunders up the steps and nearly knocks Mo
over with his fierce hug. "It's Leenie!"

The long-legged, black-haired beauty emerging from the
passenger side door is indeed her niece, Mo concedes, but
a poised, mature college student has replaced her little
"Leakin' Lena."

"It's good to see you, dear," Grammy Quinn says, giving her
granddaughter a kiss on the cheek. "You look wonderful."

"I'm fat as a pig!" Eileen says, gently hugging her grandmother, who looks tiny and frail next to her.

"The dread freshman fifteen," Mo says, stepping forward.
"On you it looks good."

"Auntie Mo-Mo! It's so good to see you!"

Mo finds herself locked in her niece's strong arms.

"Isn't anybody glad to see me?" Maddie asks as she lugs two
suitcases up the steps.

"Oh, Mama! I'll carry those!"

"What smells so good? I'm starved!" Danny says.

They leave Eileen's suitcases in the living room and herd
into the kitchen.

"I guess I won't start my diet just yet," Eileen says as she
helps Mo carry the platters of food into the dining room. "You
fixed all my favorites."

"Grammy made the meal. I was in charge of slicing and dicing."

"Shipping overchow!" Danny says—one of his dad's expressions—when they are seated around the table.

"Would you offer the grace, Eileen?" Grammy says from her place at the head of the table.

They fall silent, clasp one another's hands, and bow their heads.

"Dear heavenly Father," Eileen begins, her voice high and musical, "we thank You for this food and ask You to bless it and bless those who share it. Strengthen us in faith and love as You call us to serve you." She pauses. "Please bless and protect all those who fight to preserve freedom and especially . . ." Her voice catches. "Especially Kenny Durning. And bless and protect Aidan." She draws a breath. "Who truly needs your help and guidance."

"Amen," they chorus.

"And help me to do good in the talent show," Danny adds.

"To do *well*," Grammy amends.

"Do *well*."

"Sorry." Eileen brushes at her eyes.

"Don't ever be sorry for honest tears shed in love," her grandmother tells her.

"Pass the roast beast, please," Danny says, and the solemnity is broken.

Eileen tells them about her classes and about life in a dormitory within easy walking distance of the White House. They are halfway through their meal when a knocking at the front door interrupts them.

"I'll get it!" Danny is already up and flying into the living room.

"I wonder who that can that be," Maddie says, frowning.

"Probably those Jehovahs. They always come right at mealtime," Grammy notes.

"Gosh!" Danny exclaims from the other room as he opens the door.

A deep voice speaks, then Danny says "Sure! Come on! They're all in here!"

Thundering sneakers. Danny bursts into the dining room, shouting, "Mom!"

"Slow down, partner. You'll last longer," Grammy says.

"It's him! It's him!"

"Him who, honey?" Maddie says, getting up.

"Whoever it is, tell him we're eating," Grammy says.

A tall, well-built young man with a picket fence haircut appears in the doorway. "I'm so sorry to disturb your supper," he says, his voice soft and deep. "I was wondering if you knew where I might find Aidan."

"Hello, Rick," Maddie says, stepping forward.

The young man transfers his blue and gold SHS cap from right hand to left so he can shake hands with her. "It's good to see you, Mrs. Durning."

"You know my mother. And Danny, of course. And Eileen."

"Good to see you," he says again, nodding.

"And this, as you can probably guess, is my twin sister, Monona. She's visiting us from Wisconsin. Mo, this is Rick Sherman."

"Wow, you guys really are twins."

"That's what they keep telling us," Mo says. "It's very nice to meet you."

"Niceta meet you."

"Aidan's car's here," Maddie says, glancing at Mo. "Have you seen him today, Sis?"

"No."

"Probably still sleeping," Grammy Quinn says.

"He's out in the barn," Danny says. "In the loft. It's really neat. I'll show you!"

"Thanks, sweetie," Maddie says at the same time that her mother says, "You sit right back down, young man!"

Danny looks uncertainly from his grandmother to his mother.

Maddie puts a hand on Danny's shoulder and says, "Why don't you show Rick out to the loft and tell your brother we're having supper and that he and Rick are welcome to join us."

"Gosh," Danny says, looking wide-eyed at the quarterback. "Can you?"

"And tell Aidan his sister's here."

"Okay. Come on!" Danny herds Rick toward the door to the kitchen.

"It's very nice to meet you," Rick says over his shoulder.

"You were awesome last night!" Danny says as they cross the kitchen. "I couldn't believe we won. You…"

The outside door slams behind them.

"Good heavenly days," Grammy Quinn mutters.

"I guess Danny's a member of the Rick Sherman fan club," Maddie says, sitting down and retucking her napkin.

"Danny should finish his supper."

"I can heat it up for him, Mom. I'm sure the older boys will chase him right out."

"That's not the point!" She turns to Eileen. "Do you know this Sherman boy?" she asks.

"Not very well. He was on the student council. He seemed nice." Eileen cuts off a modest bite of her roast beef.

"This young lady was president of that student council," Maddie tells her sister.

"She knows, Mama."

"Might's well toot your own horn, dear," Grammy Quinn observes. "Nobody else is going to toot it for you."

Eileen is telling them about her freshman survey lit. course when Danny returns, Aidan with him.

"Rick said he had to go," Danny says, looking stricken.

Eileen stands and rushes over to embrace her twin.

"Hey, take it easy!" Aidan says. "You been taking steroids or what?"

"Brat!" She releases him from the hug and punches him playfully on the arm. Then she hugs him again.

When the twins stand side by side, the resemblance is striking. Aidan has his mother's wispy, blond hair, and Eileen has her father's dark Irish curls, but both are tall—Eileen is perhaps six inches shorter than her brother's 6'4"—broad-shouldered, and disturbingly good-looking, with hazel eyes and flawless features.

"Sit down and eat!" Grammy Quinn commands.

"I'll fix you a plate," Maddie says, getting up.

"I can get it, Ma. You just sit."

Aidan goes into the kitchen. Plates clatter. Eileen returns to her seat and resumes her explanation of deconstructionist literary criticism. Aidan returns, sits, and fills his plate from the platters and bowls offered him.

They wait for Aidan to finish eating, and Maddie fetches the pie and a stack of dessert plates from the kitchen. "Will you do the honors, Son?" she asks, setting the pie in front of Aidan and handing him the knife. "There's vanilla ice cream if anybody wants it."

"I'll bet even the president doesn't get pie this good," Danny says.

"I'll ask him the next time I see him," Eileen says.

"There was a president named Madison," Danny announces. "Just like my mom. We had to learn them in order in Mrs. Simpson's class. Washington, Jefferson, Adams . . ."

"Washington, Adams, Jefferson . . ." his mother prompts.

"Washington, Adams, Jefferson, then Madison, Monroe, and another Adams . . ."

Stumbling only twice, he completes the list. They applaud.

"Is that who you were named for, Mom?" he asks. "For President Madison?"

"Sure," Aidan says. "And Auntie Mo was named for President Monona."

Danny frowns. "There wasn't a President Monona. Washington, Jefferson, A . . . *Adams, Jefferson* . . ."

"Madison, Monona . . ." Aidan says, grinning.

"No! So, were you, Mom? Named after the president?"

"You want to take this one, Mom?" Maddie asks.

"I guess he's old enough to hear the story." Grammy Quinn sets her fork on the plate next to the piece of pie she's been pushing around without eating.

"When your Grandfather Quinn and I got married," she begins, "we'd planned to go to St. Paul for our honeymoon."

"I'll bet you don't even know what a honeymoon is, do you?" Aidan asks Danny.

"I do so."

"What is it, then?"

"It's a vacation people go on when they get married."

"A vacation, huh?"

"Close enough," Grammy Quinn says. "Aidan, would you like to finish the story?"

"No, ma'am."

"Yeah, Aiden!"

"Hush, both of you! We spent our first night over in Madison County, where all those pretty covered bridges are. The next morning we headed north, but your gramps got nervous about leaving the farm for so long, and we never got farther than a little town called Monona, up in the northeast corner of the state. We spent the night there, turned right around, and came home to the farm to start our married life.

"When we discovered that I was carrying twins, we decided if we had girls, we'd call one of them Madison, after where we stayed the first night, and one of them Monona, after the little town we stayed in the second night."

Danny frowns. "But why would you want to do that?"

"Told you he didn't know what a honeymoon is."

"Shush!" Eileen says, poking Aidan.

Danny mulls things over, his last bite of pie balanced on the tip of his fork. "Grampa died before I was born, huh?" he asks.

"That's right," Grammy Quinn says.

"He died four months after your Aunt Mo and I graduated from high school," Maddie adds.

"Auntie Mo? Is it hard having a funny name?"

"Aren't we full of questions, little man?" Aidan says.

"Shut up!"

"That's enough of that!" Maddie snaps. "We do not say 'shut up' in this family."

Forks clatter on plates.

"You think Monona's a funny name?" Mo asks him.

"Not funny, I guess. Just . . . different."

"You want funny. How about Eileen?" Aidan says. "It sounds like a line of cosmetics."

"And Aidan sounds like . . ."

"That's enough, you two," Grammy Quinn says. "You sound like caterwauling cats!"

"Caterwauling!" Danny giggles.

"I like having a name that's different," Mo tells him. "There were always loads of Rebeccas and Nancys in our class at school, but never another Monona."

"Remember the year we had the three Melindas?"

"Fifth grade. Sister Donald Marie kept getting them mixed up."

"You don't have any kids, do you, Aunt Mo?" Danny asks.

"No, honey. My husband has two children from his first wife."

"Did she *die*?"

"Nope. She's alive and kicking. She and the children live in Chicago."

"Are the kids my age?"

"No. They're almost grown up."

"Don't you want to have children?"

"That's enough questions," Maddie says. "You have to get ready for the talent show."

"Yeah!" He leaps up. "I'll put on my costume!"

"I'll get the dishes," Maddie says. "Mom, why don't you take a little rest?"

"I'll help," Eileen says, getting up and starting to clear the table.

"And so will Aidan."

"Hey!" Aidan yelps.

"Are you sending me to my room for a nap?" Grammy Quinn asks Maddie.

"That's right. I don't want you getting cranky later. And you get a pass on the dishes," Maddie says to her daughter. "You get to be company for a day."

"*I'll* help with the dishes," Mo says. "Your mother and I used to have dishwashing down to a science."

The family scatters. Maddie and Mo carry plates out to the kitchen, where Maddie fills both sinks with scalding hot water, the left sink for washing, the right for rinsing.

"I had a good talk with Mom while you were at the airport," Mo tells her sister as they work side by side at the sinks.

"I'm glad. Did she bring up Topic A?"

"Not a word."

"I'm surprised."

"Does she talk about it a lot?"

"Not so much any more."

"I'm sure she still thinks I'm going to go to hell for marrying a heathen."

"A *divorced* heathen at that." Maddie hands her sister a dessert plate for rinsing. "She's old school, honey, and she worries about you. I do, too, for that matter."

"Do you think I'm going to hell?"

"Of course not. But it has to make it more difficult when two people are . . ."

"Unevenly yoked? Do they still call it that around here?"

Maddie nods. "Remember the scandal when Alma Birrenkott married that Jewish man from Des Moines? What was his name?"

"Kornstein. He sold pharmaceuticals."

"Kornstein! That was it. They were the town scandal for months." Maddie plunges the roasting pan into the sudsy water and starts to scour it. "Does it?" she asks.

"Does what what?"

"Does it make things more difficult? That Doug's not a believer?"

When Mo remains silent, Maddie glances at her. "You don't have to talk about it if you don't want to," she says.

"Of course it does. I guess deep down, I keep hoping he'll see something good and beautiful in my life that he's missing, and he'll want it, too."

"In God's time, honey."

"We're very different in lots of ways, Doug and I."

"Opposites attract."

"Something like that. It sure is nice, seeing Mom so chipper today."

"Seeing you has really rallied her. I just hope she doesn't get too worn out." Maddie hands her the dripping pan. "But Aidan! He's the one I couldn't believe tonight."

"How so?"

"I don't think I'd heard him laugh since Kenny was called up. And we haven't had three words in a row out of him since the trouble started. But he was Mr. Fun at dinner."

"He just needed to see his favorite auntie." Mo dunks the pan in rinse water, takes it out, and examines it closely. "There's still some gunk on here," she says, handing it back.

"Where?"

"Right there."

"Can't you just dry harder?"

They laugh. Maddie resubmerges the pan.

"Does Aidan miss Eileen when she's away at college?"

"He does, although you couldn't get him to admit it. It was hard on him when we held him back a grade."

"Third grade, right?"

"Right. The principal convinced us that he wasn't ready for the transition from 'learning to read' to 'reading to learn.' Her exact words."

"I'm surprised Kenny agreed to it."

"I was, too. I think he felt that Aidan was being overshadowed by his superstar sister."

"She is a dazzler."

"Isn't she? She's pulling straight A's, and she's already found a homeless shelter to volunteer at one night a week."

"Any boyfriends?"

"Not to talk about. She goes to mixers, if they still call them that."

"I hate this stupid trick!"

Danny stands in the doorway, his metal rings, the size of small pizza pans, in his hands. He's wearing a tall, black hat and a red coat and tails, several sizes too big.

"What's the matter, honey?" Maddie asks.

"I can't do it!"

"You did it perfectly the other day," Mo reminds him.

"It's a stupid trick!"

"You sure look great," Mo says. "Where'd you get the duds?"

"At the St. Vincent's. It's just like the ringleader at the circus wears."

"Ringmaster," his mother amends. "And a *large* ringmaster must have worn that coat."

"Why don't we go into the living room, and I'll help you rehearse again?" Mo suggests.

"Your Aunt Mo is a great magician," Maddie says. "Her favorite trick was disappearing when the truck came to pick us up to go detasseling."

"I did not!" She turns to her young nephew. "You stay here, and when I get settled in the living room, you make your entrance."

"Okay."

The living room is cool and dark with the shades drawn. Mo

sits on the couch, her restless mind casting up anxieties about Doug and about the newspaper. Be here, she tells herself. Be now. Be what Danny needs you to be this moment. "May the words of my mouth," she murmurs, repeating the end of one of her favorite psalms, "and the meditations of my heart be pleasing to you, Oh Lord, my strength and my redeemer."

Danny enters. "What do I do now?" he asks.

"First show us that there's nothing up your sleeves. Remember?"

"Oh, yeah."

"Wait. First I'll introduce you."

Danny stands in the middle of the living room floor, the three large rings in his right hand.

"Ladies and gentlemen," Mo says. "Here, on our stage . . ."

"You forgot to say, 'Boys and girls of all ages.'"

"Absolutely right. Ladies and gentlemen, boys and girls, children of all ages! Live and direct from performances before the crown heads of India, it gives me great pleasure to introduce—Danny the Magnificent!"

Danny makes a deep bow. Then, grinning, he holds up a ring in each hand, examines them closely, then smacks them together. The two rings link.

"That's amazing!" Mo says, clapping her hands.

"It worked!"

"It certainly did."

"Wait. I'm not done."

He holds one of the linked rings in his left hand, letting the second ring dangle from the first. He holds the third ring in his right hand, again examining it closely. His tongue sticks out at the corner of his mouth. He taps the rings together, and the third ring links with the other two.

"Bravo!"

"But I won't be able to do it in front of all those people. I'll be too scared."

"It's okay to be scared. Performers are usually scared. They just don't show it."

"No they aren't."

"They are. Lawrence Olivier used to get terrible stage fright. And Johnny Carson got sick to his stomach before every show."

"Who are they?"

"Lawrence Olivier was a marvelous actor, and Johnny Carson was on television every night for a hundred years. You'd never have known to look at him that he go butterflies."

"Butterflies?" Danny giggles.

"Sure. We all get butterflies. You just have to teach them to fly in formation. Then being scared is good energy. You can use it."

"I'll bet you never get scared."

"Oh, yes I do."

"Really? When were you scared?"

The memory of facing two killers within three months flashes through her mind.

"I got nervous every time I had to interview somebody famous. I still get a little nervous just interviewing the folks in Mitchell."

"You never look nervous."

"That's the thing. You can't see my butterflies, and nobody can see yours."

"Who did you interview that was famous?"

"Julia Roberts."

"Who's she?"

"A movie star. She was in Chicago to promote a movie, but I interviewed her about having twins. I can see you're not impressed."

"I don't think I've seen any of her movies."

"How about Michael Jordan? You know who Michael Jordan is, don't you?"

Danny's eyes get enormous. "He's only the greatest basketball player who ever lived! Did you interview Michael Jordan?"

"I did."

"I'll bet you were really, really nervous!"

"That's what I'm saying."

"What did you do?"

"Wrote down three questions to ask in case my brain completely seized up, put on my game face, and did it."

"Wow! Did your brain squeeze up?"

"Nope. Mr. Jordan was very nice. He was used to having to put people at ease."

"Does my mom know you interviewed Michael Jordan?"

"Oh, yes," Maddie says from the doorway, drying her hands on her apron. "I've heard the story a time or two. Honey, we have to leave in about 10 minutes. Do you want to practice your act one more time for Auntie Mo?"

"Will you make sure I get my patter right?" Danny asks.

"Sure I will."

Turning his back, Danny disconnects the rings, then turns to face her again. "Go away," he says to his mother, who is still standing in the doorway.

"I've been asked nicer."

"Go away, *please*. We're practicing."

"Okay. Train leaves in 10 minutes."

"Will you introduce me again?" Danny asks as soon as his mother leaves.

"Ladies and gentlemen! Boys and girls, children of all ages! Live and direct from the Boom Boom room of the Bora Bora Inn in Walla Walla, Washington, the one, the only—Danny the Malodorous!"

Danny laughs. "What do I say first? I forget what you told me before."

"Say 'Hi. It's great to be here. You're a wonderful audience.'"

He frowns.

"You don't have to say that. Introduce your trick. Tell them you're pleased to perform for them an illusion first performed for the Pharaohs of Egypt."

"I'm pleased to inform you . . . What?"

"Just make up something silly to say about the trick. Say it was first performed by Michael Jordan. Anything you want. Then say, 'Please watch carefully. Notice that at no time do my fingers leave my hands.'"

"At no time . . ."

"Hold up the rings. That's right. Turn them front and back. Pass your hand through the middle. Tell them you have in your hands two solid rings."

"I have in my hands two solid rings."

"Then tell them, 'I shall attempt to do the impossible, defy-ing the laws of physics, by magically linking the rings.'"

"I shall attempt . . . I can't remember all that."

"The exact words don't matter. It's just patter. It keeps them distracted and you relaxed. And try not to stare quite so hard at the rings."

"I have to find the place . . ."

"Shh. Don't give anything away, not even to me. Magicians never reveal their secrets."

Danny nods solemnly. "I shall now link the impossible two rings," he says importantly.

"Don't forget the magic word."

"What magic word?"

"Doesn't matter. Make one up. 'Presto chango.' 'Shazam.' 'Michael Jordan.'"

"Michael Jordan!" he says, clanging the rings together. "It didn't work!"

"That's okay! Just pretend it's all part of the act. Keep pattering. Say, 'That's the first time Michael Jordan ever failed in the clutch.' Say anything. While you're pattering, you can sneak a peek at the ring."

He taps the rings, and they link. Mo claps and whistles. Danny grins.

"Thanks, Auntie Mo," he says, and runs over to hug her neck.

"You're going to be great, kiddo. Just get those butterflies flying in formation."

"Okay!"

"Better go before we go," Maddie says from the doorway.

Mo smiles as she watches Danny run out of the room. "What a great kid," she says, standing and entwining her arm around her twin's waist.

"He can be a handful."

"I'll drive in with Eileen in about an hour."

"Perfect. Better bring an umbrella. It feels like it could storm."

"Do you want me to wake Mom if she's still sleeping?"

"Let her rest. This has been a lot of excitement for her."

Mo watches from the porch as Maddie and Danny drive off. She thinks of Danny's innocent question about her not having children, and she feels a pang of . . . what? Regret? Longing? It certainly wouldn't be too late to start a family if she wanted to.

Her heart twists with a sudden ache. Here she is, thinking about the possibility of having children, it occurs to her, when she isn't entirely sure she'll still have a husband when she gets home.

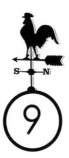

"I'm going to perform for you, 'Tomorrow,' from *Annie*, a Broadway musical based on the character of Little Orphan Annie," the little girl, introduced by Principal Sister Stella as Shirley LeVon Cooley, informs them solemnly.

With the curly hair and stage presence of another, long-ago Shirley, the poised young lady nods at the woman perched on a piano stool in front of and to the right of the stage. The woman launches her introduction, and the girl begins singing in a different key entirely. The stage light goes out. Piano and voice stumble to a halt.

"Oh, dear," Maddie murmurs, reaching over to grip Mo's wrist. "Bad start."

"Turn that light on!" a woman's shrill voice erupts from the audience.

"Sorry," a high-pitched male voice calls down from the balcony behind them.

A few folks laugh. The house lights come on, slowly dim, and go out. The stage light flares. Shirley LeVon Cooley seems not to have moved.

"I'm going to perform for you, 'Tomorrow,'" she says, in the same flat, atonal voice, "from *Annie*."

This time performer and accompanist begin more or less at the same time and in the same key. When they also end at approximately the same time, the game little girl having done her best to stay on top of her big finish, the audience responds with generous applause and a few whistles.

Mo sneaks a peak at her program. Still to come: a "comic ventriloquist," a barbershop quartet, a stand-up comedian, another singer—a young man apparently prepared to tackle "Ave Maria"—a violinist, a pianist, a flute trio. After Danny's "magical illusion" will come the grand finale, "Shaundu the Magician."

It will be a long haul, Monona decides, and the metal folding chairs in the school auditorium are no more accommodating than the ones at the Beymer Common Council meetings.

Sister Stella introduces the ventriloquist, and "Timmy O'Toole and his best buddy, Buddy" present their act. Sister Stella keeps things moving right along, and before too awfully long, the flutists are bringing a grindingly slow rendition of "Clare de Lune" to a staggering and merciful finish.

"This is it!" Maddie hisses.

"He'll be fine," Mo assures her, but her stomach, which has been knotting all afternoon, slowly capsizes.

"That was splendid," Sister Stella says, smiling at the departing flutists. "And now, Danny Durning will perform a magic trick."

Danny enters, stage right, top hat at a rakish angle, the tails of his red coat dragging behind him.

"Ladies and gentlemen!" he shouts. "I shall now perform for you an illusion that will thrill and amaze you."

"What a little ham!" Eileen whispers.

"We call that stage presence, my dear," Mo whispers back, and Maddie shushes them.

"You will not believe yours eyes," Danny continues. "For you will be seeing the impossible."

The stage light glints off the first ring, which he holds high over his head.

"You see before you a simple, ordinary ring," he assures them, passing his other hand through the center of the ring. When he lowers the ring, his coat sleeve slides down over hand and ring. He pushes the sleeve back up.

"Nothing up here," he says.

The smattering of laughter surprises him, and he grins.

"Nothing up here," he repeats, pushing up the other sleeve. "And nothing . . .," he takes off the hat and taps his head with it, " . . . up here!"

More laughter. Danny grins.

"And here," he says, "is a second simple, ordinary ring, the same as the first."

He holds his arms up, a ring in each hand. He taps the rings together once, twice, a third time, making a dull clinking sound. He closes his eyes, seeming to concentrate.

"Michael Jordan!"

He slams the rings together, and they link. The audience applauds mightily as he holds the linked rings up, and Mo hears her sister's whoosh of expelled air.

"And now," he says solemnly, "a third ring!"

When he bends over to pick up the final ring, his top hat tumbles at his feet. He picks it up, whacks it against his hip as if to get the dust off, and peers inside.

"Still no rabbit," he says, showing them the hat before putting it back on.

He holds the linked rings with one hand, the single, free ring with the other. "Michael Jordan!" he screams, banging the rings together.

But when he releases the third ring, it falls to the floor with a clank.

"Even Michael Jordan misses sometimes," he says, bending down at the knees and scooping up the ring. He takes a deep breath, casts his eyes heavenward, and again invokes the magic name, "Michael Jordan!"

This time the rings link, and he swings them dramatically by the middle ring, the light glittering off them, the rings clinking musically.

The applause is enthusiastic. Sister Stella appears at the wing, stage left, and walks into the light.

"Let's see you take 'em apart!" a gruff male voice shouts from the back of the auditorium.

"That'll cost you extra," Danny says, and the audience laughs and applauds again.

Danny bows several times before finally backing off the stage.

"There'll be no living with him!" Maddie says, but she is beaming.

"Ladies and gentlemen," Sister Stella says, "as many of you know, each year the talent show culminates in an appearance by a strange visitor with incredible magical powers. Known only as Shaundu the Magician, his true identity has never been revealed. Ladies and gentlemen, Shaundu the Magician!"

The lights go out, save for a beam directed at the middle of the stage. The beam moves slowly stage right until it encounters the curtain at the wing and begins panning back toward the other wing, as if searching for Shaundu. Someone in the audience coughs. Someone else titters.

A shower of yellow and blue light erupts from near the top of the curtain, stage center. The spotlight swings up to reveal a man dressed all in black—tights, boots, cape and cowl—descending slowly to the stage, arms spread, cape billowing.

The auditorium erupts in cheers as the mysterious Shaundu touches down on stage. Smoke from the fireworks curls out from the top of the curtain and spreads into the audience.

The spotlight finds him. Grabbing the tips of his cape, Shaundu spreads his arms and bows deeply from the waist. Thick, dark glasses mask his eyes. Straightening up, he puts an index finger to his lips. Soft flute music seems to surround him as he puts his hands together and bows his head, as if in prayer or deep contemplation. He opens his hands and thrusts them up and out, and a dove flies through the spotlight and out over the audience, to wild cheers and applause.

From the folds of his cape, Shaundu produces a gerbil, a rabbit, a chicken, and finally, outrageously, a meowing kitten, placing each on the stage at his feet, where they stare out at the audience as if mesmerized. Shaundu dips to one knee, spreading his cape over his little menagerie, until his head actually touches the stage.

When he jumps up, gerbil, rabbit, chicken, and kitten are gone.

"How did he do that?" Mo asks as the crowd screeches and cheers.

Again Shaundu places an index finger to his lips, and the audience quiets. He folds his hands and bows his head for what might be a full minute. When he finally spreads his hands, he reveals only a white kerchief, which he holds by the upper edges, showing the audience first the front and then the back. Holding the hankie in one hand, he passes the other hand over and under it. He wads the kerchief and throws it to his feet, then folds his arms and stares down at it.

"Hey, Shaundu, you dropped your hankie!" someone calls out, to laughter.

Again the index finger to the lips. Shaundu extends his hands, palms up, as if in supplication. The hankie seems to come to life at his feet, standing and twisting right and left before leaping into Shaundu's waiting hands.

The audience applauds.

The hankie begins to dance on Shaundu's upturned palm, dipping and twirling to the flute music, even seeming to pulsate with the music's rhythm. It rises slowly from his palm and dances in the air. Shaundu again passes his hand over and under the dancing hankie, then moves both hands up and down next to it. He takes a step back, then another, and the hankie continues its dance.

The music quickens, intensifies, and the dance becomes frenetic. The hankie circles the air, wider and wider, faster and faster, until, at the apex of its arc, it vanishes.

Shaundu steps to the apron of the stage to acknowledge the applause. He dips to one knee and bows, his head touching the stage, his cape covering his body.

And then he is gone.

The spotlight searches the stage, sweeping left and right, then up toward to ceiling, finally swinging out into the audience. The stage lights come up, revealing the gerbil, rabbit, chicken, and kitten sitting quietly stage front, center. The curtain drops.

"Shaundu the Magician!" Sister Stella says, walking on from stage right. The applause, which has been continuous, swells to a crescendo.

The curtain raises to reveal all of the performers in the talent show, with the exception of Shaundu. The audience stands and cheers. The curtain again drops.

"This concludes our program," the principal announces.

"I'm sure we'd like to give all of our marvelous performers another round of applause."

As the ovation diminishes, she thanks them all for coming, reminds them that rehearsals for the Christmas pageant begin in a week, and exits stage right.

"How in the world did he do that?" Mo asks, as they move slowly to the front of the auditorium with the others to wait for the performers to come out.

"I have no idea," Maddie says. "He does a different act every year, and every year, it gets more outrageous. He's good enough to be on television."

One of the young flutists emerges from the wings, spots her parents, shrieks, and runs down the stairs into her mother's hug. A stream of children follows her, the young performers expressing their relief and happiness while receiving hugs and congratulations.

"There's Danny!" Maddie pushes through the crowd to embrace her son. "You were great!" she says, engulfing the squirming young magician in a hug.

"There was a big wire!" Danny says excitedly. "And this belt thing around his waist. That's how they made him fly."

"What about the chicken and the cat?" Eileen challenges.

"I don't know *how* he did that. How was my patter, Auntie Mo?"

"Your patter was great, bud," she assures him, giving his shoulders a squeeze. "The whole act was terrific."

"What a little ham you are," Eileen tells him.

"Born to the stage," Mo says.

They head with the crowd to the side entrance.

"Did you get to meet Shaundu?" Mo asks as they emerge into the bright light of the early November afternoon.

"No! Nobody even knows who he is."

"It's Blind Ryne," Eileen says. "Everyone knows that."

"No, it isn't!" Danny shouts.

"Danny, calm down," his mother cautions.

"It isn't!" Danny insists. "Shandu is not the janitor!"

"Blind Ryne is the janitor at the school, part-time," Eileen explains. "He's the only one who can make the furnace work."

"He's really weird," Danny says.

"Danny, it's not polite to call somebody weird," says Maddie.

"'Weird' in what way?" Mo asks.

Eileen taps the side of her head with her index finger, and Danny nods.

"You don't think Shaundu is Blind Ryne, Danny?" Mo asks.

He shrugs. "I dunno. Maybe," he says, looking at his sister.

They reach the family pickup.

"I'm parked a couple of blocks away," Mo says. "The lot was full when we got here."

"Can I ride home with you, Auntie Mo?" Danny asks.

"If it's all right with your mom, I'd be honored to give the star a ride home."

"Of course it's all right. Leenie can come with me."

"I wasn't the star," Danny says seriously, as he and his aunt walk along the tree-lined sidewalk past trim two-story houses with full porches, yards neatly raked, and gardens cut back and ready for winter. "Shaundu was the star!"

"He was pretty amazing."

"I wish I knew how he did that."

They turn at the corner. Mo's car is half a block up, across the street.

"Look, Auntie Mo. Someone's trying to get into your car! And the lights are on!"

A man wearing an overcoat, hat pulled low over his face, is bending over the passenger side door of Mo's little two-seater. Hearing them, he straightens up and begins walking rapidly away.

"Hey!" Mo calls out, walking faster. Her nephew starts to run ahead.

"Whoa, Danny, you stay with me."

The man reaches the corner and slips down the side street.

"Let him go," Mo says. "He obviously doesn't want to chat."

She examines the passenger side door, which is locked, the window up.

Nothing seems to be disturbed on the inside.

"Was he trying to rob us, Auntie Mo?"

"I can't imagine. There's nothing here worth stealing."

"Maybe he just wanted to turn the lights off for you."

"Maybe." She hurries around to the driver's side, fishing the key out of her purse. "A bell is supposed to remind you to turn the lights off when you turn the ignition off," she says, fumbling the key into the lock. "But mine's broken. Doug keeps saying . . ."

She wrenches the door open, slides in under the wheel, inserts the key in the ignition. The engine roars to life.

"Thank heavens I didn't kill the battery." She reaches over and unlocks the other door for Danny, who tumbles in beside her.

"Buckle up," she tells him.

"Can we go fast?"

"This is only a Honda, buddy. She just looks fast."

Once they skirt the square and head out of town, Mo begins to relax.

"You know, I bet you're right, Danny. That man probably saw that my lights were on and was just trying to help us," she says.

"What if he *was* a burglar?"

"There really isn't anything worth stealing in here."

"If we'd caught him, you coulda beat him up!"

"Danny! What makes you say a thing like that?"

"You beat up that guy who killed your friend!"

"Daniel Patrick Durning, were you listening when I was talking with your mom the night I got here?"

Danny nods, ducking his head.

"Honey, it's not nice to eavesdrop like that.

"I didn't mean to eavesdrop. I just wasn't sleepy."

"So you snuck back downstairs and spied on us."

"I'm sorry. Is what I did a sin?"

"I don't know if I'd call it a sin, but it certainly isn't a nice thing to do."

"I'm really sorry! I won't ever do it again."

"Good."

Danny is silent for most of the rest of the ride.

"I didn't really beat anybody up," Mo says when they're almost to Durning-Quinn Road. "I just slowed him down until help could get there."

"I still think you're a hero."

"Well, thank you, honey."

But Mo feels anything but heroic. She is remembering the fear and concern in Doug's eyes that day, and how he had held her while she talked late into the night. Now he won't return her phone calls, and his two emails have been curt, even dismissive. She feels torn between staying to support Maddie and racing home to fight to save her marriage.

She pulls in at the Durning farm driveway, noticing that they have beaten Maddie and Eileen home.

Danny jumps out and races up the steps to the front door. "It's locked!" he calls down.

"Grammy must still be sleeping."

"I have to go potty!"

"Your mom will be here any minute."

"I know where there's a key. Mama keeps one on the ledge over the barn door."

He charges down the steps and around the house.

Mo walks over to the living room window and peers in. She can just see the handle of a pot on the floor through the kitchen doorway. She hurries around to the side of the house, turns over a pail, and stands on it to peer in at the kitchen window.

What she sees sickens her. The kitchen looks as if a small tornado has hit it—or at least tried to bake a cake in it. The pot Mo has spied from the living room window, along with two pans and a glass baking dish, litter the floor. A mixing bowl, chocolate chips, or perhaps raisins, an empty box, eggshells, a bottle of milk, measuring spoons and cup, and other debris engulf the counter.

The light is on over the range. The oven door is open. There's no sign of her mother.

Danny unlocks the door and steps back, smiling proudly.

"Why don't you put the key back in its place so we don't forget later?" Mo suggests.

"Okay." He studies her face. "What's the matter, Auntie Mo?"

"Probably nothing, honey." She forces a smile. "You go ahead."

"Okay."

He still looks uncertain, but he takes off at his usual take-no-prisoners gallop.

"Mom?" Mo calls as she crosses the living room, slowing as she nears the kitchen doorway.

The disarray looks somehow even more threatening than it did from the window. The stovetop radiates heat as Mo reaches to click off the oven.

"Mom?"

She hurries back through the living room to the closed door of her mother's room. She raises a fist, hesitates, knocks.

"Mom? Mom!"

She reaches for the doorknob just as the door swings open.

"Why, hello, dear. I didn't hear you come in. I was just getting ready to go to town."

Her mother has dressed up, complete with hat, purse, and dressy shoes, except that she has put her slip on over her dress.

Danny appears in the doorway. Catching sight of his grandmother, he puts his hand over his mouth and giggles.

Maddie's pickup scatters gravel as it pulls up next to the house.

"I was just getting ready to go to town," her mother says again. "Would you like to come with me?"

"Grammy! You're inside out!"

"What's that?" The older woman looks down at herself. "How about that? I guess I tried to slip one over on you."

The front door pops open, and Maddie enters, followed by Eileen. "We stopped off at the market to pick up some—" Seeing her mother, Maddie stops short.

"We have a little situation," Mo says. "Could you help Mom while I clean up the kitchen?"

"What's the matter with—?" Maddie spies the mess through the kitchen doorway. "Oh."

"I was making cookies," Grammy Quinn says, brightening. "Would you like some? They're delicious."

"Sure!" Danny says.

"Not before supper," Maddie says.

The phone rings in the kitchen and in the master bedroom at the back of the house.

"I'll get it!" Danny is already running to the kitchen.

For a moment the others just stand, listening.

"Mom! It's Dad! Dad's on the phone!"

"Good heavenly days! This place is a madhouse," Grammy Quinn says.

"Has she been like this before?"

Mo and Maddie sit on the back deck, their feet up on the railing, mugs of green tea on the small table between them. Their mother is playing hearts with Eileen and Danny in the kitchen.

"She gets confused sometimes, but she's never done anything like this. Sis, she could have burned the house down! It isn't safe to leave her alone anymore."

"Are you sure you don't have any clubs, Danny?" their mother says in the kitchen. "That's a heart you played."

"I don't, look!"

"Don't show her your hand, silly," Eileen says. "We believe you."

"Perhaps we could arrange for somebody to stay with her while you're working. Maybe Mrs. Logan could help out."

"She's a farmer's wife with three kids, honey. She's got her hands full."

"I passed a nice-looking retirement village on the way into town. It must be new. I don't remember seeing it before."

"It's been there five years. But if you're thinking about getting Mom to live there, lots of luck. She calls it 'the bone yard.' She says places like that are for old people."

"She really isn't old enough for this to be happening."

"What's the right age?"

The sun is gathering itself to slip below the horizon, its pale rays casting long, etched shadows across the back lawn but offering little warmth.

"Thanks for letting me talk to Kenny. It was really great to hear his voice," says Mo.

"He asked for you. He always asks how you're doing. I think his exact words are, 'Has your sister caught any more killers lately?'"

Mo laughs and takes a sip from her mug.

"How do you like the green tea?"

"It's okay."

"You don't like it."

"I don't dislike it. It just seems kind of, I don't know, pale."

"I can't believe you drink regular coffee after dinner. I'd be up all night."

"What can I tell you?"

"Green tea is supposed to be very good for you. Slows the aging process. You can put sugar in it if you want."

"It's fine. How often does Kenny call?"

"Every couple of weeks. He emails almost every day." Maddie leans back, taking a deep breath. "It's so strange."

"What is?"

"To hear from him like that, when he's in the middle of a war in that awful place."

"From the stories Mom and Dad used to tell, the whole country was at war during World War II. Even during the Vietnam War, everybody talked about it, demonstrated against it, rallied to support it—something. This time the soldiers are at war, but the rest of the country isn't."

"Grammy got the dirty lady!" Danny yells from the kitchen.

"What a poor sport!" his grandmother says.

They hear the sound of a slap—it hangs in the air like a gunshot. Maddie tips the table as she jumps up, the two mugs slide to the deck, and one rolls off the deck into the bushes.

Mo retrieves the mugs, dabs at the spilled tea with her napkin, and hurries after her sister into the kitchen.

"Oh, honey! Grammy's so, so sorry!" their mother is saying from her seat at the table.

Eileen has her arm around Danny, who is trying fiercely not to cry. Both stand across the table from their grandmother.

"I don't know what got into me! You know I would never hurt that boy!" She begins beating her thighs with her fists, and Maddie rushes to stop her, wrapping her arms around her.

"Why did you hit me?" Danny asks.

Grammy Quinn begins to weep, abandoning herself to heart-wrenching sobs as Mo circles her chair and kneels on the side opposite her sister. She takes one of her mother's hands and strokes it gently while Maddie talks softly to her.

A perfectly formed red handprint has blossomed on Danny's left cheek.

Still in his sister's one-armed embrace, he touches his hand to the mark absently.

At last the older woman's sobs begin to subside.

"Maybe we should get you ready for bed," Maddie suggests.

Her mother's features seem to snap into focus; her eyes narrow. "I am *not* an invalid," she says. "I do *not* need to be put to bed, by you or anyone else."

"I didn't mean—"

"I assume you meant what you said. Your father and I raised you to speak your truth!"

Withdrawing her hand from Mo's and shaking off Maddie's hug, she stands, wobbles, and holds a hand out to support herself with the table. "I am going to go to my room and prepare for bed," she says, straightening up. "I suggest you do the same!"

Mo follows her mother to the doorway and watches her cross the living room. Her mother opens her door and closes it forcefully behind her.

When Mo turns back to the kitchen, Danny is sobbing in his mother's arms.

"She didn't mean it, honey," Maddie says. "She isn't herself."

"Why was she so mean?"

"She isn't mean. Not usually. Maybe she just got too tired. How about if your Auntie Mo, Eileen, and I play hearts with you?"

"I don't want to play hearts any more."

"How about Monopoly? We haven't had a good game of Monopoly in ages."

He nods. "Okay," he says.

Maddie gets the Monopoly game out of the family room closet, and the four of them play at the kitchen table.

"I'll trade you Tennessee for Pennsylvania Avenue," Mo offers Danny.

"I'll even throw in the B&O."

"Uh-uh."

"Why not? Then we'd both have a Monopoly."

"Don't want to."

"He never trades," Eileen tells her aunt.

"But that's the fun of it," Mo urges.

Danny is adamant, and Mo settles for working out a deal with Eileen involving the low-rent properties along the first quarter of the board.

Danny soon controls Boardwalk and Park Place, the premium monopoly, and hocks all his other properties to put up hotels. Mo promptly lands on Boardwalk.

"Whoo-whoo!" Danny hollers, but then, catching a glance from his mother, he says, "Sorry, Auntie Mo."

"I can see you're brokenhearted." Mo checks her depleted stack of play money. "I'm busted," she says. "I'll give you what I've got."

Danny's face clouds. "That's okay," he says quickly. "You don't have to pay."

"Of course I do, honey. That's the rule."

"I'll borrow you the money."

Mo gets up, circles the table, and hugs her nephew, who squirms in her embrace. "That's okay, pal," she says. "I'm going to get ready for bed and read myself to sleep. All that excitement watching you perform the magic ring trick did me in."

"'Night, Sis," Maddie says as her sister bends to kiss her cheek. "Sleep tight."

"Don't let the bedbugs bite," Mo says, completing their father's old bedtime litany.

Eileen stands to give her aunt a hug.

Upstairs, Mo stretches out on Aidan's bed, where fatigue claims her. She listens to the sounds from downstairs—Danny is apparently dominating the game—and almost dozes off. Rousing herself, she gets the cell phone from her purse and speed dials her home number. After four rings, she gets Doug's voice on the answering machine.

Anger brings her fully awake. She opens her computer, logs on, and types in Doug's edress.

TALK TO ME, she types; before she can change her mind, she clicks on Send.

She starts checking her other emails. In a few minutes, the box at the base of the screen tells her she has a message from Doug.

You don't have to shout.

I'm angry, Mo types. *Why don't you pick up the phone?*

Don't like phones, the reply comes back almost instantly. *Never have.*

I'm fine, she replies. *Thanks for asking.*

I'm glad. How's your sister holding up?

Okay, considering. We had a call from Kenny. He sounded good.

This time there's a longer pause before his answer appears on the screen.

That's good. How's your mom?

Mo considers telling him about the episode and decides against it.

Distracted. She's going to need some sort of supervision soon, I'm afraid.

Sorry to hear it.

His words seem so perfunctory. Maybe it's just the coldness of typed words on a screen, she thinks. Maybe there's actual warmth, even a pulse, behind the words.

I wasn't sure you'd still be there, she types. She looks at her words on the screen. Do they sound weak? Conciliatory? Angry? How does she want them to sound?

She hits Send.

She has to wait several minutes for a reply.

Still here.

That's it? she types back. *Just 'still here'?*

She almost gives up and logs off before his reply comes back.

I moved to this godforsaken place because you insisted you wanted the simple country life. Now I'm sitting here, all alone. 'Still here' is the best I can do for now.

Mo begins to cry. The tears stop almost immediately. Suck it up, bucko, she tells herself. Get some sleep. Tomorrow's another day.

This time when she turns the bathroom fan on, the chanting that seems to bubble up under the whirring strikes Mo as truly demonic. She finishes up quickly, gets into her Lantz nightgown, and crawls into bed with her John Dunning novel, certain that she's too upset to sleep.

She awakens with the light on and the novel open, spine up, on her stomach.

The phone rings downstairs, first in the kitchen and then, almost simultaneously, in Maddie's bedroom. Mo checks her watch. 12:20 AM. This is no casual social call.

The ringing breaks off abruptly in the middle of its third iteration. The stillness that replaces it is somehow more absolute for the noise that preceded it.

After a few moments, slippered footsteps cross the kitchen and come up the stairs. Mo throws off the covers, sits up, and fights her way into her bathrobe, taking three tries to get her right arm into the sleeve.

"Sis?"

"I'm awake. Who was it?"

The door opens part way, and Maddie looks in, sleep still in her eyes. "It's Todd," she says. "Sheriff Brabender. He's still on the line. I think you'd better talk to him. There's been . . . Someone's been murdered. He says he wants to talk to Aidan."

11

"They can't possibly think Aidan killed this Grimsled," Maddie says. "Can they?"

The twins sit at the kitchen table, hunched over the mugs of green tea Maddie has brewed for them.

"If he were a suspect, they would have taken him in for questioning," Mo says, but she doubts she has quelled her sister's worry.

Everett Logan emerges from the barn, having finished milking the three cows Maddie still keeps. Danny, Chance, and Wrecker are right behind him.

When Mo had gone out to the barn to get Aidan in the night, the loft had been empty, save for the barn cats that had taken refuge from a chilly November night. But when she went back to check in the morning, Aidan had been sleeping peacefully.

"It's a stupid expression, isn't it?" Mo says.

"What is?"

"'Drug deal gone bad.' That's what Todd called it. Who ever heard of a good drug deal?" She sips her tea, wishing it were coffee.

"Yeah. I guess."

They found the body by the river, Todd had said. Grimsled

had apparently been beaten to death. Todd was guessing he had been killed somewhere else and dumped where they found him.

"Hi, Mama. Hi, Auntie Mo."

Eileen sweeps into the kitchen, still in pajamas and robe, and throws her arms around Mo's shoulders from behind.

"Hi, 'Leener. Who won the game last night?"

"Danny. He always does. What a little capitalist."

"Are you going to Mass with us?" her mother asks.

"Sure. I thought I'd log on and catch up on my soc. lecture first, if there's time. Is it okay if I use the computer in your room, Auntie Mo?"

"Of course, honey. It's your brother's room."

"You can get your lecture on the computer?" Maddie asks.

"Yeah! Isn't that too cool? It's cross-listed as a distance ed. class, and we've got students from all over the world."

"What class is this?" Mo asks.

"The sociology of third world nations. It's great. We're learning that world hunger is really a political problem. There's enough food to feed everyone, but the distribution is unfair."

Eileen pours herself a mug of tea from the pot on the table. "It's actually better than going to the lectures," she says. "The professor uses streaming video to show film clips, and all the students can post—"

"Good morning, all. What's this about a screaming video?"

Grammy Quinn appears in the doorway, dressed impeccably in the same outfit she had attempted to wear the day before.

"Mom!" Maddie rises, her chair scraping the floor. "How are you this morning?"

"Fit as a fiddle and ready for Mass."

She gives Maddie a quick hug and puts a bony hand on Mo's shoulder.

"Would you like some tea?" Maddie asks.

"I would not. I would like coffee, strong and black."

"I didn't make any. Mo's giving tea a try."

Their mother sniffs. "I'll make instant, then," she says.

"I'll make us both a cup," Mo says. "Not that the tea isn't great," she says, looking at Maddie.

"You might as well drink hot water," Grammy Quinn says.

"Never mind," Maddie says. "I'll brew a pot. I know when I'm outnumbered."

"I'll fetch the paper," Grammy Quinn says. "I see that lout of a paperboy has left it halfway to Timbuktu again."

"Danny can get it, Mom," Maddie says. "He's just finishing up his chores with Mr. Logan. The 'paperboy' is a 50-year-old father of six," she adds for Mo's benefit.

"I'll get it. I'm not an invalid."

They follow their mother through the living room and stand in the doorway to watch as she strides resolutely to the road, where the Sunday Des Moines *Register* curls like a log at the lip of the driveway.

"It's as if nothing had happened," Maddie says.

"Do you suppose she even remembers?"

"If she doesn't, it's a kindness."

They take two cars to the basilica for Mass, Eileen riding with Mo in the del Sol, Maddie taking her mother and Danny in the pickup. They arrive early; only a few folks sit scattered among the divided pews in the cavernous church. The light is on over the confession box at the back of the church, and two elderly women kneel in the back pew, saying their beads as they wait their turn at atonement.

Maddie indicates a center pew about a third of the way back from the altar, and Mo slides in, with Eileen right behind her. As

Grammy Quinn and Maddie join them, Mo sees Danny slip into the back pew next to the older women.

"What's that all about?" Mo whispers as she bends to lower the kneeler.

"I have no idea," Maddie whispers back.

The kneeler smacks the tile floor; a resounding thud echoes through the church.

"Good heavenly days," their mother says, too loudly.

"Sorry," Mo whispers. "I forgot how heavy these things are."

She sinks onto her knees and tries to pray, but her thoughts swirl among Doug, Aidan, Danny, even Shaundu, the mysterious man with the dancing hankie.

Danny slides into the pew and sits next to her. Bells jangle; two servers in cassocks march in from the side door to the left of the altar, one bearing a large metal cross, the other an ornate Bible. An elderly man in priestly vestments, his thin, snowy hair crowning his large, round head like a doily follows them, hands folded before him in prayerful attitude.

"In the name of the Father," he intones, touching his fingertips to his forehead.

Mo has already finished crossing herself before he continues, "And of the Son." His hand sweeps down to his waist. "And of the Holy . . ." The fingertips touch his left shoulder. "Spirit." His hand seems to crawl across his chest to his right shoulder.

I do hope he picks up the pace, Mo thinks. She glances at Danny, who shrugs and rolls his eyes, as if reading her thoughts.

But Father's glacial pace bogs down even more in a sermon that seems to have at least four endings before the elderly pastor stops abruptly, in mid-thought, and sits down.

When they reach the end of the rite, the priest reads the weekly bulletin to them, including the lengthy list of the parish sick. After he gives the final blessing and they are again outside, Mo is almost surprised to see the sun still short of its apex.

"I'm starved," Eileen says. "Can we go to Bev's?"

"Would hardly be a Sunday without it," Maddie says.

"Where's Danny?" Mo turns to search for her nephew in the sparse crowd lingering by the open double doors of the church.

"They have CCD between Masses. They give out cookies and punch."

"They shouldn't have to bribe the kids," Grammy Quinn says. "Learning about our Lord should be enough."

She had been cogent throughout Mass, murmuring the responses with the rest, but now she seems to be slipping again, her expression becoming worried, her eyes darting about as if she is trying to get her bearings.

The morning is warm, and Mo peels off her jacket as they walk the two blocks down Church Street and through the square to Bev's.

"Look what the cat drug in!" A woman greets them from the large circular table in the middle of the room as they enter the crowded diner.

"Come here, you," another woman at the table says, jumping up. "I'll corral a coupl'a more chairs, and you can join us."

"Sis, I guess I have no choice but to introduce you to the infamous Corny Quilters of Cowboy Country," Maddie says. "Gals, for any of you who don't know and haven't guessed already, this is my twin sister, Monona."

"Your *famous* twin sister!" says the large woman who has just purloined a chair from a nearby table. "The one who catches killers!"

Before Mo can protest, the woman slams the chair into place at the table and sticks out a fleshy hand. "Bessie Mae Snook," she says, her sweaty hand enveloping Mo's. "Formerly Bessie Mae Crabtree. You went to school with my nephew, Byerly."

"Monona Quinn," she says, retrieving her hand.

Introductions circle the table: Marcie Tupper, Joleen Vick, Alicia Pertzborn, Lorraine Otterson ("Call me 'Lollie.'"), and Patsy Nadler. The remains of breakfast sit on plates in front of each of them, the Lutheran Church having gotten out about the time the second Catholic Mass was starting.

Bessie Mae goes searching for another chair while Mo helps her mother into a chair and sits down to her left. A woman so thin as to merit the term "scrawny," wearing a wig of curly, red hair approaches, coffee pot in hand. She expertly flips over two unused mugs and pours coffee from two feet above the target without spilling a drop.

"I'll get your set-ups," she says in a low, husky voice. "You folks know what you want?"

"Better bring a menu," Maddie suggests as she takes the chair Bessie Mae has retrieved for her from across the room. "My sister hasn't been here in awhile."

"How are you, young lady?" the waitress asks Mo. "It has been a long spell."

Mo looks at the woman's face more closely, imagining it with more flesh and color in the cheeks.

"Bev?"

"Nobody else'd put up with the abuse I take around here. How you been keeping, dearie?" She sounds as if it has been two days, rather than two decades, since Mo and Maddie had stopped in almost every day after school.

"I'm fine, thanks. How are you?"

"You mean other than the g.d. chemotherapy? Not bad for an old hag."

"I'm sorry. I didn't . . ."

"That's okay, honey. I'm gonna whip the Big C, just like Cowboy Craig done. I'll scare you up a menu."

"I don't need one," Mo says. "If you still have the cowboy omelet."

"Dearie, Ned'll be making them omelets three days after he's dead. You want coffee?"

"Please!"

"Do you have granola?" Eileen asks as she settles into the fourth chair lugged by Bessie Mae.

"We got corn flakes, frosted flakes, rice krispies, and corn pops. I can throw some raisins and peanuts in if you want."

"I think I'll just have eggs, then," Eileen says meekly.

"How you want 'em?"

"Scrambled?"

"Meat?"

"Pardon?"

"Bacon or sausage?"

"Oh. No. No, thank you."

"White or wheat?"

"Do you have bagels?"

"English muffins."

"I'll have an English muffin."

"Anything to drink?"

"Orange juice?"

"Large or small?"

"Small."

"Ma'am?"

Bev turns her attention to Grammy Quinn, who has been staring off into space. She starts, blinks her eyes. "I'll have what she's having," she says.

"That it?"

"May I have a glass of ice water, please?"

"I think we can manage that. And I suppose you want tea?" This is directed at Maddie.

"Yes, I want tea."

"May I have green tea also?" Eileen says.

Bev shakes her head. "Panther pee," she says, turning and heading back to the pass-through window, where she shouts their order at the unseen cook without taking a breath.

"And two panther pees, if you please," she concludes. "Hold the crumpets."

"We were just talking about the auction," Bessie Mae says, leaning across the table toward Maddie.

"That's right, it was last night. I completely forgot."

"It was a huge success," Joleen Vick tells her, looking from Maddie to Mo.

"We took in over $5,000!" Bessie Mae says.

"Five thou . . . That's incredible!" Maddie says. "How'd we do that?"

"Over $3,000 was from one bidder," Lollie injects.

"For Alicia's Log Cabin," Bessie Mae says.

Alicia ducks her head, her cheeks coloring.

"It *is* gorgeous," Maddie says. "But $3,000?"

"I know. We couldn't believe it either. And get this. There wasn't nobody bidding against him. He just up and said $3,000, and Lollie, here, says 'Sold!' before the words were barely out of his mouth."

"I didn't want him to change his mind," Lollie says, beaming.

"Who bought it?" Maddie asks.

Bessie Mae glances around the room. "It was that janitor at the museum."

"I didn't suspect he'd have two nickels to rub together," Joleen says.

"Isn't he janitor over at the Catholic, too?" Patsy asks.

"Yep. Even two of those jobs don't add up to $3,000 for a quilt," Bessie Mae says.

"Are we talking about the man called 'Blind Ryne'?" Mo asks.

"That's what everybody calls him," Bessie Mae says.

"He certainly gets around."

"Man can't see two feet in front of him without his glasses." Bessie Mae laughs. "But be that as it may, he's okay in my book, giving us that kind of money for the fund."

"The fund?" Mo asks.

"Keep your voice down!" Joleen tells Bessie Mae. "She's standing right over there."

"It's for Bev." Bessie Mae leans forward and nods toward the pass-through at the back of the room. "To help with the hospital bills. She don't know a thing about it."

The food arrives, and Mo tackles her cowboy omelet, which is every bit as big and flavorful as she remembers.

When everyone has finished—except for Grammy Quinn, who has poked and prodded her food without eating much of it—Marcie Tupper, treasurer of the Cowboy Quilters, calculates how much everybody owes.

The diner has cleared out considerably as they get up to leave. As they move toward the door, Mo spots Luke Clausen sitting alone in a booth in the corner, a cup of coffee and a plate with the remains of eggs, sausage, and hash browns on the table in front of him. He motions her over.

"So. You heard about the grand gesture," he says.

"The grand gesture?"

"The three large Blind Ryne laid out for the quilt."

"Yes. That's really something."

"You want to know why he did it?"

Mo glances toward the door. The others are outside, standing in a large circle on the sidewalk, talking. Mo slides onto the bench across the table from Luke Clausen.

"He didn't do it out of the goodness of his heart?" she asks.

Luke laughs and takes a sip of his coffee. "He did it because he's crazy," he says.

"Crazy as in foolish?"

"Crazy as in nuts. You want some?" He points at his coffee mug.

"I'm fine, thanks."

"Hang on a minute."

The big man slides out from under the table, standing with a grunt. He crosses the room to the coffee urn in the corner by the counter and fills his coffee mug.

"So," he says when he's again settled. He throws a fleshy arm over the back of the seat and stretches a leg out on the bench. He wears the same tattered T-shirt he had on the other day, with picture and lettering so faded that Mo can make out only that it's for some sort of summer camp.

"He tell you about his book?"

"No. I haven't ever talked to him."

"He's says he's writing a book that will prove that Von Daniken was right.

"Von Daniken?"

"Erich Von Daniken. He wrote books about how we're all descended from aliens in flying saucers who visited the earth centuries ago. He claimed he had proof that Moses used a small nuclear reactor the aliens gave him to make the manna in the desert." He leans back and roars with laughter.

"That's a bit far out."

"Yeah. 'Course, nobody's ever seen a page of this great manuscript Ryne's supposedly been writing for years." He takes a sip of his coffee, and his face turns serious. "And they let this guy hang out around children," he concludes darkly.

"He sounds harmless enough to me."

"Don't believe it. You get through all that magic and the rope tricks and the rest, and there's a serious lunatic in there. I had to pull him off his buddy Grimsled the other day, or else he would have choked him to death."

"Do you think *he* might have killed Grimsled last night?"

"Grimsled's dead?" Taking his nearly full coffee mug in both big hands, Luke drains the steaming liquid as if it were water. "I hadn't heard. Can't say as I'm surprised, the kind of life he lived, but we don't get many homicides around here. Let me ask you something. Where do you think a guy like Rindeknect, who works two part-time jobs as a janitor, got the kind of dough he was flashing at the auction last night?

"I heard he was a bookmaker."

Luke nods. "He is. And he no doubt made a bundle on the football game the other night. But I think he has another source of income. Meth."

"You think he's making meth?"

"He and Grimsled. I figure they must have had a falling out, and Ryno killed him."

"And then went into town and bought a quilt?"

"Makes more sense then that business about Moses and the nuclear reactor."

Mo excuses herself a few moments later. Luke Clausen's laughter follows her out onto the sidewalk, where the Cowboy Quilters are still saying their good-byes.

12

"I can't believe it's really you!"

A smiling Lewis Crubb sits with his hands folded on the desk in front of him, the desktop empty save for computer, keyboard, telephone, legal pad, and fountain pen.

"Have I changed that much?" Mo asks from her chair across the huge desk.

"Not a bit. You're as beautiful as ever. You knew, of course, that I had a tremendous crush on you all through high school."

Mo hadn't known. She hadn't really been much aware of Lewis at all, except to know that he got all A's in honors classes, seemed to have few friends, and apparently had intended to be an attorney from the day he was born.

"Of course, you and Mr. Brabender were quite the couple, the king and queen of SHS, so I had to content myself with worshipping from afar."

"It's good to see you again, Lewis."

He spreads his arms wide. "Same old 'Huge Louie,'" he says.

He is indeed huge—easily 6'6" and 350 pounds—his fleshy face smooth and unblemished, his eyes behind the wire rim glasses sunken in flesh. His other, crueler nickname in high school had been "Pork Queen."

"You've done very well," she says, nodding her head to indicate the office, the law practice, the obvious prosperity.

"Very big fish, very small pond. The old town hasn't changed much, has it?"

"It really hasn't."

"Except for the stench. That's new this morning!"

"I noticed! What is that?"

"Dead fish. Hundreds of them, belly up in the river."

"How awful! What happened?"

"Nobody knows. The DNR's out there now, testing. I'm sure somebody will want to sue somebody over it." He laughs. "It's an ill wind, huh?" He leans forward, sliding the legal pad in front of him. "But you didn't come to talk about high school days." He sighs, as if disappointed. "Or dead fish."

"Maddie was going to get a public defender for Aidan." She takes a breath, willing herself to talk slowly. "Todd, Sheriff Brabender, doesn't think that's good enough."

Lewis picks up the fountain pen and turns it over in his hands, as if examining it for flaws before uncapping it. "What else does Sheriff Brabender say about the case?"

"He thinks Aidan's covering for somebody else."

"Does he have any idea who that someone might be?"

Mo shakes her head and then, realizing that Lewis is taking notes and not looking at her, she says, "No." She waits for the pen to stop its slow, stately sweep across the pad.

Lewis looks up, heaves another sigh. "I specialize in corporate law. I have clients in Des Moines, Omaha, and Lincoln, even a couple up in your old stomping grounds. I do wills, estate planning, that sort of thing, for some of the folks in town here.

But I haven't defended someone in a criminal case since Mother's brother, Thomas, got arrested for mail order fraud."

"Would Aidan's case be complicated?"

"How old is he?"

"He's 18."

"This is his first offense?"

"That's right."

"And he was in possession of how much marijuana?" He pronounces the word as if it were distasteful to him.

"I'm not sure. Just a couple of ounces, I think."

"You think."

"He hasn't talked about it."

"Not to anyone?"

Mo shakes her head. Again she waits while Lewis makes his careful notes, the letters sweeping and rounded. He dots each "i"with a circle.

"The legal issues," he says finally, capping the pen and placing it squarely in the center of the pad, "are not at all complicated. He should be given a fine and some sort of community service—picking up trash along the highway, that sort of thing—and placed on probation for six months, maybe a year."

"Should be."

Lewis picks up the pen, again examines it, and places it back precisely where it had been. "Iowa has been fighting the war on drugs for some time," he says, "and drugs appear to be winning. Rather decisively, actually.

"Instead of changing tactics, the powers that be have decided to wheel out bigger weapons. Our local D.A., Tommy Halleron—he was two years ahead of us in high school—seems to be bucking for a battlefield promotion. Rebecca Barrows is an able and fair-minded jurist, but she, too, has little tolerance for drug usage, especially when it involves young people."

"Are you saying that Aidan could go to jail?"

"I'm saying that he could face tough sledding in court."

Mo waits, but Lewis seems to have nothing more to add.

"Can you... Would you help him? Help us?"

The counselor takes a deep breath, holds it, lets it out. "I certainly would," he says, "but I'm not sure I can."

"Why not?" It comes out louder than she intended.

"If the young man isn't confiding in his immediate family, it's highly unlikely that he would confide in me. Under the circumstances, I'm not sure what I could do that a competent P.D. couldn't."

"But whatever you did, you'd do it better. Wouldn't you?"

Lewis allows himself a small smile. "Yes." He nods. "I imagine I would."

"Then please take the case. I'd be able to pay you, although not all at once."

"This isn't about money."

"I wouldn't expect you to work for free."

"And I wouldn't accept money. Not from you."

Mo can think of nothing to say to that.

"Will you have the young man call me to make an appointment?" Lewis says at last. "If he's willing to extend himself that much, I'm willing to do what I can."

"Thank you!" Mo is out of her chair and leaning across the huge desk to shake her former classmate's hand, which is like a pillow.

"Don't thank me yet," he says.

She hears these words again in her mind as she walks across the square.

They seem to take on an ominous tone, although the lawyer's voice had been pleasant enough.

Don't question it, she tells herself. Just thank God he'll take the case.

At the museum, Maddie is waiting to show her the recent improvements.

"All of these saddles were part of Mr. Marvel's estate out in Thousand Oaks, California," museum curator Garley Payne tells her as the five of them—volunteers Debra Myklebust and Milfred Muskett have also come along—take in the new additions to the collection.

"He wore every one of these outfits in his movies," Debra tells her as they review the glass cases housing the sequined, richly appliquéd shirts, leather pants, and hand-tooled boots Cowboy Craig favored later in his career—when his activity had become pretty much limited to fairs, parades, and rodeos.

But Mo loves the fringed black buckskins and black boots, scarf, and Stetson of the original Cowboy Craig, star of Beymer Studio serials and, later, the TV series that made him a kids' hero for over a decade. She pauses to examine the displays of newspaper articles, stills, and movie posters that trace his life from small town Iowa boy to star.

Cowboy Craig's horse, Mercury, the golden palomino with the "flashing hooves and the fighting heart," billed as "the bravest horse in the old west," merits a room of her own, its walls covered with posters and photographs of the great horse's exploits. In the center of the room, Mercury herself rears for all eternity on her back legs, front legs pawing the sky—not a statue or replica but the horse herself, or at least the hide and the best taxidermy money could buy.

It would have been only slightly creepier if a stuffed and mounted Cowboy Craig sat atop her, hat doffed and raised to the adoring crowd.

"Can you come back this afternoon?" Milfred asks when they finish the tour. "A group of school kids is coming in for a demonstration of trick roping."

She points to a poster on the wall announcing the next performance of "The Range Roper," complete with picture of a grinning, masked cowpoke twirling a rope with one hand, a pistol with the other.

"That's our Mr. Rindeknect," Garley Payne tells her. "He's our janitor and handyman, but it turns out he has talents we hadn't imagined when we hired him."

"He's such a nice man," Milfred adds. "So good with the kids. They just love him."

"Maybe another time," Mo says. "And thank you so much for the tour. You're really doing a wonderful job. The museum is a treasure."

"If you'd like, I'd be happy to take you through the boyhood home," a beaming Garley Payne offers.

"Maybe another time," she says again.

"Of course. What was I thinking? You've no doubt seen the place a hundred times."

If not a hundred, at least a couple of dozen, including school field trips of her own. But there had been no Range Roper to perform for the kiddies then, and no Shaundu to thrill and amaze the crowds at student talent shows.

Is there no end to this Rindeknect's talents, she wonders as she and Maddie walk to Maddie's pickup in the museum's dirt parking lot out back. Who exactly is this man, who can apparently be all things to all people? By all accounts, he's a bookie, he might be involved in drug trafficking, might even be a murderer; and yet folks trust him to entertain their kids and hang out at the Catholic grade school?

When they get back to the farmhouse, Eileen is packed but seems reluctant to leave.

"I'll be back at Christmas," she promises. "I have my cell with me all the time. And you can always email."

"We'll be fine." Maddie gives her daughter a hug. "You just keep up the good work."

"I wish I could have spent more time with Aidan, but he seemed—I don't know. Every time I got in the same room with him, he looked for a reason to leave."

"I'm not going to the airport," Grammy Quinn announces from her bedroom door.

"But I thought we were all—"

"I'm tired. I'm not going."

"But I—"

"It's okay, Sis," Mo says, gently touching her sister's elbow. "I'll stay. I can get some work done. And that way, someone will be here when Danny gets home from school."

"*I'll* be here!" Grammy Quinn insists. "I'm not going."

It's settled—Mo stands on the porch waving as the pickup carrying Maddie and Eileen turns around in front of the barn and heads down the long driveway.

"Good-bye, Auntie Mo-Mo," Eileen calls out the window. "I love you."

"I love you, too!" Mo calls back.

She remains on the porch as the truck passes out of sight and until even the sound of its engine fades. When she gets back inside, she finds her mother sitting in the rocker in the living room, hands folded in her lap.

"Can I get you anything, Mom?"

"No, dear. I'm fine, thank you. Where are the others?"

"The . . .?"

"Maddie and, and . . ."

"Eileen?"

"Yes, of *course*, Eileen."

"They just left for the airport. Eileen has to get back to school."

"Nobody told me."

Mo swallows an answer and retrieves her laptop from Aidan's room. She plugs it in and runs a long cable to the Internet hookup in the alcove at the base of the stairs that serves as the farm office, so she can sit on the couch near her mother and work. She retrieves her email and begins editing pieces Vi has forwarded for this week's *Doings*.

"Could we have the radio on, please?" her mother asks after awhile.

"Of course. What would you like?"

"Are you sure it won't bother you?"

"Not at all. I'm used to working amidst chaos."

"Classical would be nice."

Mo turns on the living room radio, which is already tuned to the FM public radio station in Ames, and a violin concerto fills the room.

The rocker squeaks. Her mother's eyes droop. Her head sags, her mouth falls open, and she begins to breathe deeply, making a soft wheeze when she exhales. Mo gets up quietly and goes to her mother's room to fetch a shawl to cover her.

A scrapbook lies open on the bed, exposing a page of yellowing newspaper clippings, one including a very old picture of a very young Monona over the headline:

SUMMERFELD YOUTH SCORES IN 99TH PERCENTILE IN STATE READING TEST

The other two stories on the page give accounts of a piano recital in which Mo had fought her way through *Fur Elise* and a grade school play in which Mo had the lead.

The tape holding the newsprint to the page is yellowed and brittle. Mo turns the page carefully, then turns another, and her early life passes in review. There are other plays—she was Marian the Librarian in *Music Man* and Maria in *The Sound of Music* in high school—stints on the Student Council, and her coronation as Homecoming Queen, with Todd Brabender her King.

As she carefully folds back the pages, she sees herself go off to college, intern at "an internationally known magazine in Chicago" (the *Pentagram* had refused to identify the magazine as *Playboy*), receive her degree from Northwestern. Here, too, are some of her earliest stories in the *Tribune*. She doesn't remember having sent them to her mother, and yet here they are, page after page of them, and then many of her columns, including the one in which she announced that she was leaving the paper.

She turns the page to discover the story from her first issue as editor of the *Doings*, in which she proclaims herself to be "eager to meet all of you and willing to work hard to provide the kind of community newspaper you can be proud of."

The stories of the two murders are there, of course. But her mother has also saved many lesser stories, features Mo wrote about the Fireman's Park, the Fourth of July parade, the old woman who carefully preserved her husband's basement model train layout after his death.

Mo knew her mother had kept a scrapbook for her, and one for Maddie as well, but had no idea that she'd kept it up after Mo had left home.

Her mother is snoring when Mo returns to the living room. Mo carefully spreads the shawl over her mother's shoulders and lap and repositions her head to try to keep her from getting a stiff neck.

She sits on the couch, computer on her lap, and watches her mother sleep.

Warmth washes through her as she remembers the stern but loving woman who raised her and her twin, insisting from the beginning that they were two very different individuals and refusing to dress them alike. All those years, Mo thinks sadly, when I barely kept in touch, feeling that she was somehow punishing me for leaving.

Mo returns to her work. Her mother is still sleeping when Danny charges up the driveway from the bus. The Catholic school doesn't have bus service, Maddie had explained, but the public school bus driver, Marge Langston, gives Danny a ride home on days when Maddie works her second job at the museum.

"I'm home!" Danny announces as he hurtles across the living room and nearly crashes into his aunt, who shuts the laptop and gives her nephew a hug.

Grammy Quinn starts awake. "Who's that?"

"It's me, Grammy! Your little tornado boy!"

The older woman straightens up, wincing with pain. "Why

did you let me sleep so long?" she asks Mo. "I've got to see to the chores."

"What chores?" asks Danny.

Mo puts a hand on his shoulder, and he looks a question at her.

"Got to see to things," Grammy Quinn says vaguely. "Put things right. Got to get the pies in the oven."

Fearing a repeat of yesterday's kitchen disaster but not wanting to hover, Mo decides to move her computer into the kitchen and continue to work. When her mother becomes absorbed in thumbing through her old recipe box, Mo goes back into the living room to check on Danny and finds him sitting in the wing chair by the front picture window.

"Whatcha doing in there?" he asks.

"My homework."

Danny giggles. "Adults don't have homework."

"I wish."

"Can I see?"

"Sure."

Mo fetches her computer. Danny plunks himself on the couch next to her and peers at the screen.

"What's that stuff?"

"This is Alma Peterson's correspondence from Red Rose."

"What's Red Rose?"

"A general store, a church, and a few dozen houses about 15 miles from where I live."

"Who's Iris Bamburger?"

"A nice lady who lives in one of those houses. Her grown-up daughter and her family just visited all the way from Roanoke, Virginia."

"Who cares about that?"

Mo laughs. "Iris Bamburger, mostly. Some of the other folks who live in Red Rose. A few others who used to live in Red Rose or nearby."

"What are you doing to it?"

"Editing."

"You fix the spelling and stuff?"

"Yeah. And stuff."

"Does anybody ever get an 'F'?"

"I don't give them grades. Sometimes they let me know if they don't like a change I've made, though."

"Auntie Mo? Can I tell you something?"

"Of course you can." She closes the laptop and sets it on the couch beside her. "Just a second. Let me check on something first."

Grammy Quinn is still sitting on the stool in the kitchen with her recipes stacked in piles on the table, a look of fierce concentration on her face.

Mo returns to the couch.

"What's on your mind?" she says.

"You said eavesdropping isn't a sin, right?"

"It depends on what you do with the information you overhear."

"You mean like not telling anybody?"

"Yeah. If telling would hurt the person."

His face clouds.

"Is there something specific you want to talk about?"

He looks away. "The priest said that, for my pennants, it would be okay if I told you instead of Mom."

"Penance. Tell me what, honey? Did you eavesdrop again?"

He nods, his face solemn.

"Who did you eavesdrop on?"

"Aidan. And Rick Sherman."

"That day he came looking for Aidan when we were eating supper?"

"Yeah. I didn't mean to. I just heard things while I was going down the ladder."

He is near tears. She slips her arm around his slender shoulders and gently draws him closer. "Would telling what you overheard hurt Aidan?"

"I don't know. I don't think he'd want me to."

"Would *not* telling hurt him?"

"I don't *know*!"

"Shhhh. It's okay, honey. Let's just think this thing through, okay?"

He nods. Tears roll slowly down his cheeks. Mo gives him a gentle squeeze of encouragement and waits.

"Rick sounded real mad."

"What did he say?"

"He said Aidan should 'sit tight.' And not worry."

"Not worry about what?"

"I don't know."

"Did he say anything else?"

"He said, 'Everything will work out all right.'"

"But you don't know what he meant?"

Danny shakes his head.

"Did Rick say what would happen if Aidan didn't 'sit tight'?"

Danny again shakes his head. He begins to cry in earnest now. Mo hugs him with both arms and rocks. When the crying slows, she digs a tissue out of her sweater pocket and holds it for him while he blows his nose.

"You did the right thing, telling me," Mo says when the crying is mostly finished.

"Is Aidan in more trouble?"

"I don't know, honey. But whatever's going on, we'll help him. Isn't that right?"

Danny nods. "The priest says I have to say a whole rosary for my pennants. Penance."

"I'll pray it with you if you want."

"Really?"

"Sometimes I pray the rosary when I don't even have to."

"Why do you do that?"

"It just seems like a very good thing to do."

"I'll go get my rosary."

"I'll wait right here."

Danny charges through the kitchen and upstairs, the order in his universe restored. As she gets her rosary out of her purse, Mo wishes she could restore the order in hers. So far, nothing seems clear, except that the people she loves most are hurting, and she doesn't seem to know how to make any of the hurt better.

13

"How in hell we ever used this old pisser is beyond me," Harold Joseph says, scratching a tuft of wispy, gray hair. "But by golly, we did it. Got the scars to prove it."

He hoists the rolled sleeves of his soiled, white shirt, revealing the splotchy burn scars running up both arms.

He and Mo stand at the ancient Linotype machine that squats in the corner of the Summerfeld *Pentagram* office.

"I can't imagine how anybody ever came up with the idea for this thing," Mo says.

"Musta been old Nick himself. An instrument of torture's what it was."

"But certainly faster than setting type by hand."

"I dunno 'bout that. I was pretty damn fast in the day. Got so I could compose right on the stick. Read better upside down and backwards than I could forwards." He chuckles, then digs at the tuft of hair again with his knuckles, making Mo wonder if he might have sanded off much of his hair that way and was just now finishing the job.

He leans down to give the Linotype a pat, and three cigars

fall from his shirt pocket to the floor. He picks them up with a grunt, his other hand grabbing at the small of his back.

"Damn, getting old's a bitch."

Mo almost laughs, so exaggerated is the mournful look on his long, basset-hound face. "You never actually printed with this, though, did you?" she asks, stepping over to the hand printing press, its platen smooth and shiny from decades of black ink.

"Sure did. Still do, for job printing. Folks like to have their business cards done letterpress, so you can feel the letters." He rubs index finger and thumb together. "A poet here in town has me print up 50 copies of his stuff on cover stock. He gives 'em away to anybody who'll take 'em."

"But the newspaper is printed somewhere else now?"

"Oh, yeah. Central plant's up in St. Joe's. They print maybe a dozen weeklies up there. Mine's far from the biggest. That the way you do?"

"Yes. I don't think the building's had a working press in it for 20 years."

"Ain't much else to show you. Come into the back room if you wanna. That's where we do layouts."

Three-foot-high stacks of newspapers line all four walls of the smaller inside room. Two large, slanted light tables, both covered with scraps of paper, dominate the middle of the room. The front page is being laid out on the first table. Under the *Pentagram* banner, a huge, eight-column headline proclaims:

LOCAL MAN FOUND DEAD: SHERIFF SUSPECTS MURDER

"Big news this week, huh?" he says from behind her. "You still lay 'em out this way?"

"No. We do all our layouts on the computer now."

The veteran editor whistles through his teeth. "Ain't that something? No more scissors and glue."

"Nope."

"You probably don't need a darkroom either."

"Pictures go right from the camera to the printed page."

"You don't fool around with 'em, do you?" He winks. "Put one gal's head on another one's body, like that magazine did?"

"No. We haven't decapitated anybody yet. At least not on purpose."

"You don't have all those damn chemicals to get rid of, either."

"Right."

"Sometimes I'm tempted to just cart 'em over to the river and dump 'em. I'd never do it, though, not like that son of a buck who killed all the fish."

"Is that what killed the fish? Chemicals?"

"Can't think of anything else it would be, this time of year."

"Any ideas as to who might have done it?"

"Sure. Whoever's making that meth."

He leads her back into the front room, shoves a pile of papers aside, perches on the edge of his desk, and gestures for Mo to take the lone chair. He takes a cigar out of his shirt pocket, examines it, and bites off the end. He leans down, no doubt to spit the end into the waste basket, thinks better of it, and turns his head slightly while he spits the end into his hand before dumping it. He jams the cigar in his mouth and fishes around on the cluttered desk until he finds a loose kitchen match, which he lights by snapping the tip with his thumbnail. The flame flares; the smell of sulfur makes Mo's nose twitch.

"You mind?" He holds the flame a few inches from the cigar.

"No. I like cigar smoke, actually."

He draws the flame to the tip of the cigar, opening the side of his mouth to let puffs of smoke escape. He shakes the match out and flicks it into the wastebasket, which brims with discarded paper.

"Your husband smoke?"

"No! He barely consents to breathe the air." It's out before she knows she'll say it.

Harold Joseph laughs, and Mo feels her cheeks flush with embarrassment.

"What I mean is, he takes very good care of himself. Gets lots of exercise, watches what he eats."

"Sounds like a pain in the ass. You used to smoke."

"That's right. Two packs a day."

"Unfiltered, I'll bet."

"How'd you know that?"

"Just a guess. You wrote for the Chicago paper."

"For the *Tribune*, yes."

"Used to be a damn fine paper."

"Used to be?"

"Yep. Used to mean something, that they run the American flag in the banner. Damn shame, what's been happening in this country, don't you figure? Drugs, gambling, all manner of idiocy. And I'm talking right here in Falkner County." He takes a long draw on the cigar, turning his head to expel the smoke.

"Now we even got a murderer running around loose. Not that that Grimsled character didn't have it coming. But I guess you know all about people getting murdered."

"The two people killed in Mitchell hardly 'had it coming.'"

"But some folks do need killing, don't you figure?"

Mo decides the gnarly old editor is simply trying to get a rise out of her and doesn't take the bait.

"Guess I may as well wake this damn thing up." He leans over and plugs a loose cord into the back of the phone on the desk. "Damn thing drives me buggy. Can't think straight with it ringing all the time."

"Don't you need to take phone calls?"

He shrugs, takes a reflective drag on the cigar. "Folks call back if they really need something." He shoves to his feet with a grunt and puts the hand not holding the cigar to the small of his back.

"You want, we can exchange papers," he says. "Ain't anything in mine most weeks, but I'd be curious to see what you fill yours with. Weeks when you don't have a murder to write about, that is."

He walks her to the door, then stands, blocking the doorway, his hand on the knob. "Gotta be that buddy of his done this one, don't you figure? That Blind Ryne character."

Not waiting for an answer, he steps aside and opens the door for her.

"Nice chatting with you," he says.

"It's very nice meeting you," Mo says.

The door closes behind her with a soft click.

As she walks across the square, the courthouse clock strikes the half hour. With a few minutes to spend before she's to meet Maddie at Jill's Quilts, she stops in front of Profitt's Hardware and scans the sign in the window.

FARM TOYS

ANTIQUE FARM IMPLEMENT MUSEUM

tours by appointment

Clabe Profitt, prop.

A bell over the door jangles as she enters. A cash register that might itself be an antique sits unattended on the counter to the left of the door.

Seeing no sign of antique farm implements or toys, Mo

walks down one of the narrow aisles, between high shelves crammed with tools, feeds, poisons, and paints.

The floor creaks beneath her feet. When she stops at the end of the aisle, the silence buzzes softly in her ears.

"Help you?"

Clabe Profitt emerges from between the shelves two aisles over.

"Just browsing," she manages. "I was wondering about the antiques."

"Keep 'em in back. Show you if you want."

"Thank you. I'd like that."

He leads her to a door at the back of the store. A scrawny, weathered man with an apparently permanent squint, even in the dim light of the store, he could be wearing the same overalls she saw him in at the football game. The same or different pieces of painted wood stick out of his breast pocket, and the same seed cap perches on his head.

He draws a ring of keys from his pocket, shakes out the one he wants, and inserts it in the lock. He steps aside to let her enter first. The room is larger than she expected and filled with all manner of machines and gadgets, some of which she recognizes as earlier versions of the tools she grew up with on the farm.

For the next 20 minutes, he provides a running commentary: here a cradle reaper, there a manure spreader, and over here, a one-row, horse-drawn planter. Like the Linotype, these implements strike Mo as both crude and ingenious.

Stepping around an ancient reaper, Mo discovers two rows of shiny, new toy tractors, complete with John Deere and McCormick emblems.

"This here's your John Deere pedal tractor with front loader. Let you have it for a hundret fifteen dollar. Wouldn't be making a nickel." He scowls at her. "If you was in the market, that is," he says.

They work their way to the back of the room, where a miniature farm, including two-story house, barn, out buildings, and animals, covers a table stretching the length of the back wall.

"I fiddle with this when I get the time," he says from behind her. "Always something needs doin'."

He picks up a tiny wooden hay wagon, turns it over to examine it, and sets it back down. Several models, in various stages of repair, clutter the end of the counter.

"Look at this here." He picks up a tiny tractor and rubs the wheels against the table several times with short, choppy movements. When he sets it down, the tractor wobbles across the table with a soft whir. "Friction powered," he says, almost smiling.

Mo drifts over to a side table, where she picks up a jigsaw puzzle box. "We had this one when I was a kid," she says.

"That stuff ain't for sale."

He snatches the box from her and puts it back in its place with the other puzzles, board games, and books. He glares at her, and she fights the urge to look away.

"Come on, then."

He herds her back out the door and locks it behind them.

"Thank you for the tour."

He dips his head, turns, and slips between two shelves, leaving Mo to show herself out.

Back on the street, she tries to shake off a definite case of the creeps.

Now she has to hustle to get Maddie, and together they walk to the school to escort Danny and the rest of the fifth and sixth graders to the Majestic, where Sister Stella has arranged for a special matinee showing of *The Sound of Music*.

The kids buy their snacks and scramble to fill the first three rows, a teacher or parent corking the ends of each. Mo sits on the left aisle of the third row. As she waits for the lights to dim and the show to start, she tries to remember the last time she has been in the "Mighty Majestic." Could it have really been high school, nearly 20 years before?

The old girl has maintained her tottery dignity, at least if you overlook the paint peeling from the high, vaulted ceiling, the tatters in the curtain, and the many light fixtures that now emit only blank stares. The smell of stale popcorn pervades, and Mo's shoes already stick to the floor goo.

She turns and checks the crying room and the smoking room at the back, both dark now. A beam of light explodes from the tiny window of the projection booth, dust particles dancing in its currents.

The kids cheer. The soundtrack for a Pepsi ad blares, and blurry images loom over them on the screen. It takes the projectionist a moment to get the sound below the threshold of pain and the picture into focus.

The feature begins, to wild cheering; the hills are again alive with the sound of music, and the sisters again worry about what to do about Maria. The kids are restless in some parts, but overall remarkably well behaved. The real-life sisters clearly maintain firm discipline.

Danny talks about the movie as he, Maddie, and Mo walk to Maddie's pickup, parked in the alley behind Jill's. The sun has already slipped behind the buildings on the west side of the square, and the air is cooling rapidly.

"If Eileen were here, she'd be 'deconstructing' the plot," Maddie says.

"I think it's wonderful, how enthusiastic she is about her classes."

"Oh, I do too. I just worry that a little knowledge can be a dangerous thing."

"'Drink deeply,'" Mo finishes the quote. "'Or taste not the Pierian Spring.'"

"What's that?"

"Alexander Pope. I read it in college, back when I was doing my own deconstructing."

"I wouldn't know anything about that."

Mo glances at her sister but can't read her expression. "My car's on the other side of the square," she says when they reach Maddie's pickup. "I'll meet you at home."

"Can we have pizza for dinner?" Danny asks.

"Sounds good to me," Mo says. "Why don't you let me get it? Auntie's treat. Is that local place, Lombardo's, any good?"

"Yeah!" Danny says. "Get pepperoni!"

"How about half and half?" Maddie negotiates. "Pepperoni and veggies."

"Thick crust!" Danny says.

"Whole wheat," his mother counters.

"Deal."

"Got it," Mo says. "Half and half, pepperoni and veggies, whole wheat, thick crust, and lots of mushrooms all over everything."

"No!" Danny howls. "No mushrooms!"

While she waits for the pizza at Lombardo's, Mo sits at a table by the window, leafing through a discarded copy of the *Register*. The phone rings steadily with take-out orders, but the rest of the small dining area is empty.

Mo wonders if there might have been resentment in Maddie's comments.

After all, Mo had been able to go away to college and get her degree while Maddie stayed on the farm, taking a few vocational classes at the tech school. She had always seemed happy and fulfilled in her roles as farm wife and working mother, and Mo had even envied her at times. But Maddie has had to shoulder so many burdens—the farm, Aidan's troubles, and their mother's deterioration, along with the constant worry of Kenny being in Iraq.

"Quinn?" The skinny teenager with a blond cowlick who took her order eyes her from the counter. "Your pizza's ready."

Mo pushes her thoughts aside and hurries to get the pizza home while it's still hot.

Mo awakens in darkness. On this moonless night, Aidan's room looks no different with eyes open than with them shut. They have forgotten Danny's nightlight, and in his movie-induced exhaustion, he has gone to sleep anyway. She gets out of bed, fights into her bathrobe, gropes her way to the door, and, still disoriented by sleep, creeps down the short hall to the bathroom.

The laboring banshee fan emits a high-pitched wailing over a low, constant moan. She promises herself she'll take the thing apart and spray it with WD-40 tomorrow rather than endure one more such concert.

"Home repair is simple," Doug told her once. "If it doesn't move and it's supposed to, use WD-40. If it moves and it isn't supposed to, use duct tape."

The memory makes her heart ache. Before going to sleep last night, she had again exchanged terse emails with her husband, feeling the huge gulf between them in his civil but clipped responses. As soon as they had a court date set for Aidan, she would drive back home, even if it meant a return trip to be with Maddie for the trial. It wasn't that long a drive, for heaven's sake. It isn't like they live on two different planets.

It just seems that way.

A bumping noise makes her start, and for a moment she sits still, straining to hear. Just more of the fan's cacophony, she decides.

When she snaps off the light and opens the bathroom door, the darkness is somehow more compelling, the silence deeper. She clicks on the hall light to guide her back to bed.

She freezes. With the light has come a sudden sensation of movement suppressed—something, or someone, downstairs.

You're just spooked, she tells herself. More of that intuition Doug is so fond of teasing her about. She starts down the hall to the stairway, her nerves screaming. Pulling her bathrobe tightly shut and belting it, she steps onto the top stair, then the next, avoiding the third stair, which creaks, and staying near the wall, where her steps are less likely to make any sound.

She pauses at the landing. Seven more steps to the right and then another landing and right for the final three steps into the family room.

On the third of the seven steps, she freezes again, certain she has heard, or sensed, something. She forces herself to take a slow, silent breath. Lord Jesus, she thinks, watch over me and help me to do Your will, now and always.

She reaches the second landing. The light from the upstairs hall throws soft shadows into the deep gloom of the family room. She counts slowly to 10, takes a step, counts to 10 again, takes the second step. And the third. She is standing in the family room.

Her hand brushes the wall to her right, seeking the light switch. When she finds it, she hesitates, then clicks the switch up, bathing the room in light.

She screams before she knows what she's seeing, a shadowy form first sensed at her sight's periphery, then seen fully as it darts to the door.

"Hey!" Mo shouts. "Hold on!"

The form plunges out the door and into the darkness. Mo races across the room and throws the wall switch, flooding the deck and yard with stark light.

The figure runs across the yard, taking short, choppy steps, scales the waist-high log fence, and disappears into the blackness of the fields.

Something touches her, and she almost screams again.

"What is it, Auntie Mo?"

She looks down into Danny's frightened face. "We had a visitor," she says, fighting to keep her voice controlled.

"Wow!" Danny's eyes are enormous. "We better call the cops!"

"Yeah," Mo agrees. "We'd better."

14

Mo and Maddie are taking inventory in the family room when a car turns in at the driveway, the headlights throwing moving shadows on the wall.

"He's here!" Danny screeches, charging in from the living room.

"Hold your horses, there, buster," Grandmother Quinn says from the rocker. Her voice is flat, her face expressionless. She wears an old, tattered terry bathrobe over her nightgown, and her short, gray hair looks like brambles.

Danny shadows Mo and Maddie out onto the porch as Todd gets out of the car, his 6-foot-plus frame seeming to unfold from the Dodge in stages. Although he couldn't have had more than a couple of hours' sleep, he seems "starched and pressed," as their mother might put it, as he crosses the yard, his face composed in careful non-expression.

"You're sure he's gone?" he asks before he even reaches the porch.

"Aunt Mo chased him off!" Danny says.

"Hardly," Mo says. "But I'm pretty sure he's long gone by now."

"He was in the house?"

"Yes. In the family room."

"Everybody's alright?"

"Yes. We're fine."

"Anything missing?"

"We're checking now," Maddie says. "It doesn't look like it."

"I'll take a look out back. Show me exactly where he went."

"Sure," Mo says, falling into step as the sheriff bounces down the stairs and walks briskly around to the back of the house.

"He ran straight across the yard to the fence and out into the field."

Todd takes a notepad from his back pocket and flips it open. "Did you get any sort of description?"

"Not much. He wasn't very tall, maybe 5'7", and slender."

"You're sure it was a man?"

"Well, no, actually. I just assumed."

Todd nods, making a couple of slashes in the notebook. "Okay," he says, flipping the book shut and jamming it back in his pocket. "I'm going to take a look around out here. I doubt I'll find anything, but it doesn't hurt to check."

"Can I go with you?" Danny says from behind Mo.

Todd pulls a large black flashlight off his belt and snaps it on. "You take your Aunt Mo back inside and look after things until I get back," he says. "Can you do that for me?"

"Okay," Danny says, trying not to sound too disappointed.

"Lock all the doors," Todd says. And then, catching Mo's look, he adds, "Just in case."

Mo is pouring her second cup of coffee when a tap on the window of the kitchen door makes her start. She flips on the porch light, and Aidan turns his face away from the light. He's wearing jeans and a sweatshirt. His hair is rumpled. He rubs at his eyes.

"What's going on?" he asks when Mo opens the door. "I heard somebody out back. Is that the sheriff's car?"

"Yes. We had an intruder."

"An intruder? You mean, like, a burglar?"

"We don't know what he was after. Todd, the sheriff, is—"

Someone raps on the front door, and Mo carries her coffee into the family room, Aidan following, where Maddie unbolts and opens the door for Todd.

"Did you find anything?" she asks.

"Some footprints out by the fence. Pretty nondescript. I doubt they'll help much."

He walks over to where Mo and Aiden stand in the doorway.

"Hello, Aiden."

"Hello, Sheriff. I guess we had some excitement, huh?"

"Were you here at the time?"

"Yes, sir. Out in the barn."

"You didn't hear or see anything?"

"No, sir. I must have been asleep."

"He can sleep through anything," Maddie says.

"Hmmm. Been here all night?"

"Yes, sir." He glances toward his mother.

"Any idea how he got in?" Todd asks Mo. "There's no sign of forced entry."

"No."

"I'm sure I locked up," Maddie says. "At least I think I did."

Todd nods. "You folks try to get some sleep," he suggests. "I'll come back out when it gets light and take another look around. Oh, and make sure all the doors are locked."

Maddie and Mo walk him to the front door and onto the porch. They stand side by side on the top step as the Dodge backs down the drive, swings out onto the road, and, with gravel pelting the underside of the car, roars off.

Good as his word, Todd comes back an hour after sunrise. Grandmother Quinn is in her room, presumably asleep, and Aidan is in the barn, where he went shortly after the sheriff left. Danny and Mo are playing Crazy Eights at the kitchen table while Maddie cleans up after breakfast.

"Any news?" Maddie asks as she lets Todd in at the kitchen door.

His expression and the way he hesitates before answering reactivate Mo's alarm, sending a slight electric charge through her. She stands and walks over to her sister.

"Have some coffee?" Maddie asks. "I've got a fresh pot brewed."

"Where's Aidan?" Todd asks.

The words send a stronger jolt through Mo.

"Out in the barn," Maddie says, her eyes searching Todd's, she, too, alerted now. "Getting ready for school."

"I'll go get him!" Danny says, popping up.

"That's okay," Todd says, too quickly. "I'll get him."

Mo feels her heart pound and tries to brace herself. Lord Jesus, help Maddie to bear whatever comes, she prays.

"What's happened?" Maddie manages.

Todd glances at Danny.

"Danny, you go get ready for school."

"I am ready for school."

"Then go help Mr. Logan with the chores. I'll call you when it's time to go."

"Do I have to?"

"Yes, you have to. Scoot."

"I need to ask Aidan some questions," Todd says as soon as Danny has gone.

Mo feels Maddie sag next to her and puts an arm around her waist.

"There's been another murder," Todd says.

Mo tightens her grip on her sister's waist.

"Ryne Rindeknect. We discovered his body about an hour ago in the meth lab we've been looking for. We got a tip from a neighbor who heard shouting from what she thought was an abandoned barn nearby."

"What does this have to do with Aidan?"

"We need to talk to him. See what he knows about this. We found something . . ." Todd reaches into his shirt pocket and brings out a coin. He holds it out in the palm of his hand for them to see. It is a shiny Sacachewea dollar.

"We found this near the body. Aidan showed me one just like it once."

"You think Aidan killed Ryne?" Maddie's voice rises and nearly breaks.

"We just want to talk to him. At this point, we aren't drawing any conclusions."

Again Mo and Maddie stand together on the porch as they watch Todd walk Aidan from the barn to the car. Todd hasn't cuffed him. Aidan's head is down, his shoulders slumped. He doesn't look at them as he ducks his head to get into the car. Todd shuts the door and walks around to the driver's side, nodding to them before getting in and backing down the long driveway.

"Oh, my God," Maddie moans.

They go in and sit at the kitchen table.

"What do we do now?" Maddie asks.

"I'll call Lewis Crubb. He can be at the sheriff's office by the time they get there."

"Yes. I guess he'll need—"

"What's going on?"

Their mother stands in the doorway, hair disheveled by sleep, her bathrobe hanging open over her nightgown.

"We have a situation, Mom," Mo says, taking her by the shoulders and leading her to the table. "Maddie will get your coffee while I make a phone call."

"What kind of a situation? Why are you herding me like a sheep?"

"Let's get the radio on," Maddie says. "*Morning Edition.* Your favorite."

"Why are you treating me like an idiot? Where's the newspaper?"

Mo uses the phone in the master bedroom. She skims the slender phone directory underneath the nightstand by the bed, finds the number and quickly punches it in.

"Lewis L. Crubb, Attorney at Law," a prim female voice answers on the second ring.

"This is Monona Quinn. May I speak to Mr. Crubb, please?"

"This is Mr. Crubb's answering service. Is this an emergency?"

"Yes," Mo says without hesitation.

"Please hold the line."

Thankful not to be assaulted with easy-listening music, Mo sits on the bed. She hears her mother's raised voice from the kitchen, then Maddie's softer, placating murmur. Their mother had always been so sunny in the morning, her cheerfulness in sharp contrast to their laconic, slow-moving father.

"This is Lewis Crubb."

"Lewis! It's Mo."

"What's up?"

"Todd's bringing Aidan in."

"Is Aidan being arrested?"

"Todd says they just want to talk to him."

"Do you know what about?"

Mo realizes she'd assumed Lewis would already know. She steadies herself before continuing. "There's been another murder."

"Good God. Who?"

"Blind Ryne."

"What makes them think Aidan had anything to do with it?"

"They found a coin. They think it's Aidan's."

"A coin?"

"A Sacachewea dollar, like the one his father gave him."

"I'll get right over there. Can you meet me at my office at, say, 9:30?"

"Of course. Thank you. Thank you so much."

"That's quite alright. And Mo? I know it sounds idiotic to say, but try not to worry. And try to keep Maddie as calm as possible. So far, Aidan's just what you folks in the fourth estate call a 'person of interest.' They'll have to charge him with something or let him go, and they'll need something more substantial than a coin to hold him."

"Okay. Thank you."

Lewis breaks the connection. Mo starts to recradle the phone, then speed dials her home number. When she gets the answering machine, she says, "Doug? There's been a murder. Another murder. The sheriff took Aidan in for questioning. We're meeting with an attorney this morning. I'll keep you posted."

She almost hangs up before adding, "I love you, Doug. Bye."

The phone rings as Mo walks back into the kitchen.

"Good heavenly days," their mother says from the table. "This is a madhouse!"

Maddie snatches up the receiver. Her face clouds in confusion.

"Doug? It's me. Maddie. Just a second. Mo's right here."

She hands the phone over. Mo takes it, turning her back on them. "Doug?"

"What murders?"

"Two men who were apparently involved in drug trafficking."

"And they think Aidan killed them?"

"They haven't charged him with anything."

"Good God."

"I'll know more after I talk with the attorney," Mo says. "I'll call you then. You will pick up, won't you?"

"Yeah, I'll pick up."

Her hand trembles as she hangs up the phone. It rings almost immediately; she jumps.

"Hello?"

"Mo? Please, please be careful."

"I will. Doug, I . . ."

"You don't have to catch every murderer. Okay?"

"I know. I just . . ."

"I understand. You're standing by your sister and your godson, which is exactly what you should be doing. Just try not to get hurt doing it."

"I will."

The line goes dead again.

"I'm coming, too," Maddie says. "To talk to Lewis."

"Maybe it would be better if you tried to keep things as normal as possible," Mo says, nodding toward the kitchen table, where their mother is chewing a piece of dry toast. "Take Danny to school and go to work. I'll look after Mom, keep the appointment with Lewis, and see if they'll let me in to talk with Aidan."

"I can't just pretend none of this is happening."

"You don't have to pretend anything. Just keep on keeping on until we see what we need to do next."

"We can't leave Mom here alone. Especially not with that prowler on the loose!" The button she has been worrying on her dress comes off in her hands. "Oh!" She thrusts the button in her pocket. "I'll ask Everett to stick close to the house this morning. He's got plenty to do around here."

Mo studies her sister's face. Maddie has always been strong and resolute, accepting life's vicissitudes. But now she looks very close to the edge. Mo puts a hand on each shoulder. "We'll get through this. Okay? Just like always. You and me and Jesus."

Maddie nods, brushing away a tear. "That's what you said when Kenny took that disgusting LeAnn Anderson to the junior prom."

"And I was right, wasn't I?"

"Yes."

"If you survived that, you can survive anything."

Maddie almost laughs.

"You just listen to your sister. I'm older and wiser than you."

"You're seven minutes older."

"And those seven minutes make all the difference in the world, kiddo." Mo gives her sister a quick hug. "Remember what Dad always used to tell us?"

Maddie nods. "Knock the peewadden out of them."

"That's it."

"Did you ever figure out what a 'peewadden' is?"

"Nope. Never did."

"Me, neither."

The sisters embrace once more and turn together to face the day.

The receptionist shows Mo into Lewis Crubb's office immediately when she arrives, a little before 9:30.

"Aidan says he doesn't know how the coin got there," the attorney says when she is settled in the chair across the desk from him. "He says he wasn't anywhere near any meth lab, last night or ever."

"Have they arrested him?"

"No. I think Todd just wants to hang onto him until he can check a few things out."

"How does it look?"

"All they've really got is that coin. It doesn't help that Aidan was recently arrested for possession. It also doesn't help that he can't produce the coin his father gave him."

"I know it's not supposed to matter, but do you think Aidan did this?"

"Who says it isn't supposed to matter?"

"Isn't that what lawyers always say on television?"

Lewis snorts. "Television." He leans forward and folds his hands in front of him on the desk. "It matters to me. It matters a hell of a lot. And no, I don't think Aidan killed anyone."

He looks down, the confidence momentarily gone from his round face. "I've of course advised Aidan not to say anything more unless I'm present. I did, however, consent to let them take a DNA sample from Aidan."

He looks up, his smile almost rueful. "If they find Aidan's DNA in that godforsaken barn, it would be a very bad thing," he says.

Mo reports briefly to Maddie at Jill's Quilts and heads back to the farm.

As she turns onto the county road that will take her to Durning-Quinn Lane, a vague premonition grips her, and she urges her little car on as fast as the rural road will allow.

Everett Logan is standing on the front porch when she pulls up to the house. He waits for her to get out and climb the porch steps.

"Now, here's just the damnedest thing," he says without preamble, twisting and untwisting the oily rag in his hands. "I was puttering around, close to home here, like Maddie said to, checking in on Mrs. Quinn every now and again?"

"Yes?"

"I didn't want to be obvious. No offense, but your mama's got herself a temper. She'd give me a real good tongue lashing if she knew I was keeping track of her like that."

Mo fights the urge to take the man by the shoulders and shake the story out of him.

"Last time I saw her was, oh, maybe 15, 20 minute ago. She was in the kitchen, like she was getting ready to do some baking. She caught me looking in at her, and so I just waved and went about my business."

"Where is she now, Mr. Logan?"

"Well, that's just it. The thing of it is, when I went to look in on her just now, I couldn't see her in the kitchen. So I went inside? To check the rest of the house?"

"And . . .?"

"It's the damnedest thing, like I say. But she ain't here. Not downstairs, not upstairs, not in the basement, not no place. She's just up and gone."

15

Mo's first instinct is to call Maddie. She has the phone in her hand and is fishing through the directory for the number of Jill's Quilts when she begins to reconsider. Calling Maddie now would accomplish nothing and would surely upset her terribly. Her twin is very close to what Kenny refers to as "breaking down the corral fence," as it is.

Mom might simply have gone for a walk, Mo tells herself. Any minute, she might come charging up the driveway, elbows flaring out, head down, the way she always takes on the world.

Or she might have become confused and gotten hopelessly lost. She might even have fallen and hurt herself.

Or whoever was prowling around in the night might have come back.

Oh, please, dear God, let her be safe!

Mo cradles the phone and runs down to the end of the driveway to look both ways along Durning-Quinn Road. A gentle breeze stirs the tenacious leaves in the oaks, and white puffs of cloud roll toward the horizon in a soft blue sky.

Mo runs back into the house and punches in the number for the sheriff's office.

"Sheriff of Falkner County."

"Is this Tiffany?"

"Yeah. Who's this?"

"Monona Quinn. We met the other day."

"Yeah. I remember."

"Is Sheriff Brabender in?"

"Naw."

"What about Deputy Lampere?"

"He's here."

"May I talk to him?"

"Sure. Just a sec." Tiffany apparently doesn't bother putting her hand over the receiver, and Mo can clearly hear the exchange.

"Pick up on line one!"

"Who is it?"

"Mrs. Durning's sister."

"Who?"

"Mrs. Quinn. Aidan's aunt. She was in here the other day."

"What's she want?"

"She didn't say. You want me to ask her?"

"No. That's okay. I'll take it."

After a brief pause, she hears the deputy say, "It isn't working."

"You pushed the wrong button again."

A moment later, the phone makes a soft popping noise in her ear. "Yes? This is Deputy Lampere. What can I do you for, Mrs. Kin?"

"It's my mother. She's not here, and I'm a little concerned."

"Why's that? You think maybe your prowler came back and got her?"

"The thought had occurred to me," she says, stifling the urge to add, "you moron."

"How long's she been gone?"

"Just a few minutes. I'm concerned that she might have become disoriented."

"You want me to come out and take a look around?"

"I'd appreciate that. And could you please let Sheriff Brabender know the situation?"

"I can handle this, Mrs. Kin."

"I'm sure you can, Deputy. I'd just like to make sure Sheriff Brabender knows."

"Sure. I'll tell him. You just sit tight. We'll have your mama back in no time."

Mo checks the barn, looking for Everett Logan. She goes back inside and calls her old home phone number, praying that Mrs. Logan will be inside to pick up.

"Hell-o."

"Mrs. Logan?"

"Yeah. This Monona? Mercy, but you sound just like your sister."

"Mrs. Logan, have you seen my mother?"

"Call me Emmy, dear. Everybody does. But no, I haven't seen her all day."

"Could you do me a big favor?"

"Sure will if I can."

"Can you come over, just for a little while? I'm going to look for her, and I want to be sure somebody's here in case she comes back while I'm gone."

"Is everything all right? I hear you had yourself some excitement over there last night."

Mo wonders briefly which "excitement" she's referring to.

"I'm sure everything's fine," she says. "I'm just a little worried about Mom."

"I'll be over in two shakes of a lamb's tail, honey. You just sit tight."

True to her word, Emmy Logan wobbles up the driveway on one of her sons' battered bicycles a few minutes later. Mo runs down the porch steps and meets her in the yard.

"I thought maybe you'd want to take the bike. Cover more ground that way."

"Thank you. I haven't ridden in awhile."

"You know what they say about riding a bike."

Emmy slides off. Mo grabs the handlebars and swings her leg up over the seat, feeling the muscles on the inside of her thighs protest.

"You can adjust that seat if you need to. Anything I can do for you while I'm here?"

"No. Thank you. Just keep an eye out for Mom."

"Will do, honey. Where's that husband of mine?"

"He's checking the fields in back. He said she wanders out that way sometimes."

"You might try up by the cemetery. She liked to walk up that way, too, before her arthritis got to hurting her so much."

"Thank you. I'll try there first."

The old balloon-tire bike bumps along the rutted dirt drive. By the time Mo reaches the road, the final shards of her composure have been rattled out of her. She stops to get her bearings, then pushes off, the tires slipping on the gravel.

She pedals slowly, the bike wobbling at the slow speed, while she scans both sides of the road. Without much momentum, she has to push hard on the pedals to keep the bike moving. She totters through the left turn onto Cemetery Ridge Road, hearing the eerie, familiar sound of geese passing overhead. She stops to scan the sky until she spots the uneven "V" heading southwest.

The cemetery seems deserted, but Mo drops the bike and walks the length of one of the rows of gravestones, just to be sure. Satisfied that the cemetery is empty, she pedals slowly out past the great woods of her childhood adventures, coming first on the Sorenson farm and then the Palmer Brothers spread. "The best tended farm in seven states," the brothers, Elmer and Marvin, always used to boast. The bachelor brothers had seemed ancient when Mo was in high school.

Could they still be alive? The farm is certainly still neat and tidy; someone has even raked the dirt behind the back stoop.. Laundry flaps lazily on the line, taking advantage of whatever heat the pale sun provides. The overalls on the line make Mo think the brothers still live there.

She presses on until she has to admit to herself that she's gone much farther than her mother could have possibly walked. She pedals back to Durning-Quinn Road, feeling more confident on the bike now, and heads left, north.

Failing to find her, and with a fluttering in her heart and apprehension rising to a low howl in her head, she doubles back past the Durning farm driveway and makes a similar cast south.

Nothing.

When she admits she might as well head back, she turns the bike too sharply in her frustration, violently wrenching the handlebars, and falls on her right side, the bike on top of her. It happens so fast, she has time to think only, "I'm falling," before slamming into the hard-packed dirt. Stinging pain shoots through her hip, and gravel digs into her cheek as she lies, stunned, taking inventory to see if all her parts are in working order.

Fairly sure she hasn't broken anything major, she untangles herself from the bike and stands, her hip throbbing and burning, her shoulder beginning to register its own complaint. She picks up the bike and begins trudging back along the road, her hip hurting too much to let her try to remount.

Birds chirp, leaves flutter, and white clouds roll heedlessly toward a horizon they can never reach. Their silent perfection seems to mock her desperation. She pushes herself to walk faster, the bike bouncing along in the ruts and erosion lines in the road.

Long before she reaches the driveway, she sees the brown Dodge tucked up against the side of the farmhouse. Despite her pain and the clumsiness of pushing the bike, she breaks into the fastest trot she can manage.

Her mother and Randall Lampere are sitting in the living room, the coffee pot between them on the low table, beside a plate of Pepperidge Farm Chocolate Chunk cookies, the only "store-bought" she ever serves.

"Hello, dear," her mother says as Mo closes the door behind her. "Do you know our Sheriff Lampere? He came by for a little visit. Isn't that nice?"

"We've met." Randall Lampere awkwardly stands and then finds himself with no place to put his hands.

"The sheriff was just telling me about a most distressing rise in the use of dangerous narcotics among our youth. It's all really quite unmooring."

"I really should be going, Mrs. Quinn," the deputy says, "now that your daughter's back."

"Must you? We were having such a nice chat."

"I enjoyed it, ma'am. And thanks for the coffee and cookies."

"You're very welcome." She begins to struggle up out of her chair.

"I'll see him out, Mom," Mo says, and the older woman sags back into the chair with a huff of exhaled breath.

"I found her out in the fields behind the house," Deputy Lampere says as soon as the front door has closed behind them. "She didn't have a notion where she was."

"Thank you so much for finding her."

"I don't want to butt in or anything." He plants his Mountie-style hat firmly on his head and tips it back with his index finger. "But you gotta get her outta here and into the home, and I mean PDQ. Your mama's losing it, and if you don't do something, she's gonna wind up hurting herself and maybe somebody else, too."

16

"It doesn't feel right," Maddie says. "Being here."

"Here" is high in the bleachers, on the home team side at Francis Sprengle Field, home of the fighting Summerfeld High School Cowboys, where the local heroes are attempting to dump the undefeated Fort Dillon Mustangs and earn the right to vie for the state championship.

Mo leans over, her hand light on her sister's arm. "I know," she says.

"But it's good for Danny to be here."

They have decided to go to the game to keep things as normal as possible for Danny, who, despite the absence of his big brother on the field or in the stands, appears to be completely absorbed in the action on the field.

That action consists of star quarterback Rick Sherman mixing runs and short possession passes to drive his offense steadily down the field toward what seems an inevitable touchdown and an early lead.

"Scoring first would be a huge psychological advantage," Everett Logan assures them, "in a game with so much riding on the outcome."

Everret's wife is home with Grammy Quinn, and the three stairstep Logan boys sit to their father's left, never taking their eyes off the field.

With a second down and short yardage on the Mustang's 37-yard line, Sherman executes a beautiful play action fake, seeming to hand the ball off to his halfback for a plunge into the center of the line but then tucking the ball against his right hip and rolling out to his right. A wide receiver, Kevin Mason, fakes a short curl pattern and sprints straight down the sidelines toward the goal line. With a Fort Dillon linebacker bearing down on him, Sherman fires the ball downfield. It arcs in the stadium lights, a perfect, tight spiral, gliding over the defender's flailing hands to cradle softly into Mason's waiting arms. Without breaking stride, the tall, willowy receiver glides into the end zone for the touchdown.

"Will you look at that!" Everett hollers, turning to pound the closest available son on the back. "That was beeeeeeeee-U-tiful!"

Mason flips the ball casually to the referee before being engulfed by his teammates as the home crowd roars.

But the cheers die too soon. Instead of lining up to attempt the extra point, the confused players look back up the field, where Rick Sherman lies crumpled near the Cowboys' bench, the team trainer down on one knee beside him, the coach hovering over them both. The referee sprints back up the field, signaling for an officials' injury timeout.

Silence chokes the bleachers on both sides of the field. In the stillness, the murmurs of the trainer's voice drift through the stands like smoke from a nearby campfire. A train sounds its whistle at the crossing at Main and Water.

Mo says a quiet prayer for the boy, who has yet to move. Maddie puts a hand on Danny's shoulder, and he turns and buries his head in his mother's side.

The Cowboy players circle their quarterback, so that it's impossible to see if he's responding. The ambulance that has been parked behind the south end zone makes its cautious way out onto the field. Two attendants leap out, doors slamming almost simultaneously; the circle of players parts to let them in.

Moments later, one of the attendants, a short, muscular black man, reemerges and sprints to the back of the ambulance, where he extracts a gurney and wheels it back.

The two assistant coaches herd the players to the bench. The attendants carefully strap on a collar to stabilize the injured boy's neck before sliding their arms under him and easing him onto the gurney. Sherman's arm slides off his body, but Mo can't tell if the movement is voluntary or simply the result of gravity.

Applause swells as fans on both sides of the field salute the fallen warrior. The gurney makes its short journey to the ambulance, and the attendants cradle their burden and slide it into the back of the van.

Russell Sherman emerges from the stands and sprints awkwardly toward the ambulance. No one tries to stop him. One of the attendants has followed the gurney into the van, and the other has slammed shut one of the double doors when the elder Sherman reaches him. They talk for a moment, and the attendant nods. Russell Sherman tries to climb into the van. The attendant forms a cradle with his hands for Sherman to step into, and boosts him in.

The young black attendant, his bare arms glistening with sweat, closes the second door and trots around to the driver's side of the van. The ambulance turns in a wide circle, its lights making a slow arc across the opposite side stands, and creeps through the end zone and out into the night. The mournful siren pierces the night stillness and keeps up its steady wail until it fades out of range.

The coach manages to get eleven players onto the field to attempt the extra point, but the kicker shanks the ball, missing the uprights, wide left.

Danny weeps softly. Maddie turns so that she can wrap her arms around her son, and Mo puts a hand on his shoulder and squeezes gently.

"Hey, don't count us out!" Everett leans in to tell him, reaching out a broad, callused hand to ruffle the boy's hair. "We ain't licked yet."

As Mo tries to fall asleep that night, her hip throbs with pain, her shoulder hurts every time she forgets and rolls onto it, and her face stings. But those superficial wounds aren't what keep her from sleeping.

She worries for her sister. How will Maddie bear up under all the burdens God seems to have placed on her? One son in jail, the other struggling to understand; a husband at war; a mother drifting into dementia; a farm needing constant tending.

And a sister who doesn't seem to be able to help her with any of it.

Since Mo left Chicago, death has seemed to stalk her. First Charlie, the gentle café owner, and then Father O'Bannon, the soft-spoken priest, are murdered in her once-peaceful adopted hometown of Mitchell. And now two seamy characters living on the edges of her sister's life die sudden, violent deaths.

She hasn't been "playing detective," as Doug accuses her. But her emotional ties to the first two victims and her job as editor of the community newspaper drove her to solve both murders in Mitchell. In the process, she placed a great strain on her fragile marriage, and now Doug isn't even sure he can continue to live with her.

She helps solve other peoples' problems, but she can't solve her sister's—or her own.

She thinks of the crowds taunting the crucified Christ. "You saved others," they yelled. "Why can't you save yourself?"

Anger burns away tears. You're wallowing in self-pity, she rebukes herself. Comparing yourself to Christ! And the notion that you're somehow responsible for the evil you've encountered is nonsense.

You're not helpless; you will act.

And do what?

When trying to track down a complicated story for the *Trib*, Mo learned to go directly to the source most closely involved and ask the difficult questions. She faced down politicians, athletes, entertainers, business leaders, felons, and con artists, gaining a reputation for her ability to get people to talk, especially when they didn't want to.

Now, she realizes, she must face down her own nephew.

Aidan had so far resolutely refused to talk to anyone, including his mother, about his involvement in the web of drugs and death that now threatens to ruin his life. She must get him to reveal his secrets.

Resolution replaces remorse. She will talk to Todd and then to Aidan tomorrow morning. She will learn his truth, whatever it may be, and the truth will set him free.

Or convict him of murder.

No! The light of truth shining on Aidan's darkness cannot hurt him.

And now, resolute and with a plan, Mo can at last sleep.

Somewhere near dawn, she dreams she is walking on a dirt

path through a pine forest, hand in hand with the man she loves. Sunlight filters through the trees. Birds sing, and jays call to each other from tree branches. She gives the man's hand a squeeze, and when he squeezes back, it's as if an electric shock passes through her.

They emerge into a meadow, knee deep in grasses and wild flowers, a profusion of color and life. The wet, spongy ground yields beneath her feet. Soft mud oozes cool and rich between her toes. The trees at the far side of the meadow cast long shadows as the sun slips behind them.

She is naked, the ground firm, soft, and dry beneath her. Her lover caresses her, his hand weightless. Her skin tingles, and she arcs to his touch. His lips find hers. She feels his weight on her, and yet he is somehow light, airy; her body seems to merge with his. He penetrates her, and she opens up to him, warm, liquid, two becoming one as he moves in her. His passion explodes in her, and she gasps as spasms of pleasure shock her until she is sure she can endure no more.

It is becoming light. Too soon. Too soon. How can the night be over? She struggles to hang onto the dream, caught between sleep and wakefulness. A dog barks close by. She hears voices. She is awake, in Aidan's bed, in her sister's house. Wrecker is barking outside her window. Danny and Chance are laughing. She gets up, grabs the bathrobe draped over the desk chair, puts it on and pulls it close around her, her shoulder shrieking with pain.

She stands at the window, watching as Chance throws a tennis ball to Danny, with Wrecker chasing after it. Danny catches the ball deftly, and Wrecker slams to a stop, tail wagging, eyes intent on the ball. Danny fakes a throw, and Wrecker charges wildly after a phantom. He turns, confused, and begins to lope back toward Danny, who winds and fires the ball over Wrecker's head, and over Chance's outstretched hands as well, setting off a wild chase. Wrecker easily outdistances his young master, grabbing up the ball and setting off down the driveway, the boys in laughing pursuit.

She smiles. She has been dreaming. A good dream. Specific memory is gone; only warmth remains.

But when she thinks of the job facing her that morning, the warmth dissolves, and she steels herself against what she must do.

The warm feeling returns as Mo turns right off Durning-Quinn Road onto the county road leading into Summerfeld. She struggles to remember the dream but again has only a vague awareness of wellbeing.

Don't examine it too closely, she tells herself. The feeling at least temporarily takes the edge off the anxiety that floods her every time she thinks about where she's going and what she's going to do.

"May the words of my mouth," she murmurs, the end of the nineteenth Psalm, "and the meditations of my heart be pleasing to You, oh Lord, my strength and my redeemer."

She continues to pray silently as she passes the familiar landmarks on the western side of town—the ramshackle Trail's End Motel and the Early Bird Diner; the abandoned drive-in movie, its huge screen still looming over fields of weeds; a tiny pond where she and Maddie swam as kids.

With a rare morning off and exhausted by her labors and by grinding anxiety, Maddie is at home with Danny and Grammy Quinn. Mo told her she needed a few things at the pharmacy and offered to pick up anything the family might need. But she turns left onto Church Street at the west side of the square and drives directly to the sheriff's office.

"'Lo, Mrs. Quinn." Failing to stifle a yawn, Tiffany looks up from the textbook open on the desk in front of her.

"You practically live here."

"Sheriff's giving me extra hours. I told him I needed the money for Christmas. He's real good about that." She glances back at her textbook, frowns at the passage she's been wrestling with, and again focuses on Mo.

"What happened to your face?"

So much for cover-up cream. "I fell off a bike."

"Oh, good. I mean, not good, but I thought you might have been, you know, assaulted or something. What with everything that's been going on and all."

"No. Nothing like that."

"Too bad about the game, huh?"

"Yes. Were you there?"

"Sure. Wasn't everybody?"

"Just about. Have you heard anything about Rick Sherman's condition this morning?"

"Nuh-uh. Last night they said he was conscious and wasn't paralyzed or anything and that maybe he just had a real bad concussion."

"I hope it's nothing more serious."

"Yeah. You want coffee?"

"No, thanks. I'm coffee'd out for now."

"'S'pose you wanna see the sheriff?"

"If he's here."

"Talk about somebody living here."

She gets up and saunters toward the back, hips swaying in a way Mo imagines must haunt the dreams of the high school boys. She catches herself wondering if Todd has taken note of the movement. The office door is ajar. Tiffany raises a fist to tap on the frame, but Todd appears, filling the doorway. Even from across the room he looks tired. She's surprised to see that he isn't wearing his uniform but instead clean, well-worn blue jeans and a light blue, long-sleeved shirt.

"Mrs. Quinn's here to see you?"

"Thanks, Tiffany."

His smile seems forced as he crosses the room. "Hey," he says, stopping a few feet away from her.

"Hey. You're not regulation today."

"Casual dress Friday."

"It's Saturday."

"Right. You want a cup of coffee? We can talk in my office."

"I'd like to talk with Aidan."

He nods. "I hope you have better luck with him than I have. He hasn't been very talkative with me."

"Maybe he'll listen, then."

"Don't know as he's doing much of that, either. Hard to tell."

"He might open up to me."

Todd nods again. He seems distracted, but then, he would have a lot on his mind. "You haven't seen any more of our prowler friend?" he asks.

"No. It's as if he just vanished." Like Shaundu's handkerchief, she thinks.

"Nothing was missing?"

"Not that we can tell. There is one thing . . ."

"What's that?"

"I caught somebody poking around my car downtown. After Danny's talent show."

"Poking around?"

"He might have been trying to get into the car. I'd left the lights on, and I thought he might be trying to turn them off for me."

"Did you get a good look at him?"

"No. He ran off."

"But you think he might be the same person you saw in the house?"

"He could be. I thought I should mention it."

"Good. I'm glad you did."

"Do you have any leads on the prowler?"

"Not really. If we catch him, it'll either be because we get lucky or because he does something really stupid. It's not like on television."

"Todd, I really think Aidan will talk to me. May I see him?"

"Of course. By rights, he shouldn't even be in jail."

"I don't understand."

Todd leans forward, hands folded on his desk, eyes intent on Mo. "We don't have enough to arrest him, but I'm convinced that he knows something, that he's protecting someone. I figured letting him stew in a cell overnight might give him a chance to think things through."

Mo starts to protest, but Todd holds a hand up. "I just want what's best for your nephew. Come on. I'll walk you to the jail."

Todd is silent on the short walk from the sheriff's office to the Town square, and Mo lets her mind range over several possible explanations for the events of the past few days. As they turn the corner onto the square and the Falkner County Courthouse comes into view, she notes that if someone wanted to make a movie set in small-town America in the 1950s, he could hardly find a better venue.

The jail annex is little more than a four-celled holding pen for drunks and vagrants. Her nephew sits in one of those cells, hunched over on a concrete slab jutting from the wall, his head down, his hands hanging between his knees. He wears the clothes he was picked up in, jeans and a white dress shirt, the sleeves rolled to his elbows.

The door clangs shut behind her, sending a shiver through her.

The cell is bare save for a toilet in the floor in the corner, a steel button in the floor next to it, and a small, water-stained sink on the far wall.

No sharp objects, Mo thinks, not even a toilet handle that could be pried off and used as a weapon—or as a means of self-destruction.

She forces the thought from her mind.

"How's Mom doing?"

She finds Aidan's eyes on her; he looks away. "She's worried."

He nods and again looks at the floor. He makes a low noise deep in his throat.

"What's that?"

"I didn't say anything."

"Sounds like you're catching a cold."

"It was cold in here last night."

"Did Todd—Sheriff Brabender—tell you what happened to Rick Sherman last night?"

His nod is barely perceptible. He makes another growling noise.

"Did you say something that time?"

He clears his throat. "Sorry. I said, 'Yeah.'"

"Tough break, huh?"

"Yeah."

"Word is he might only have a very bad concussion. I guess that's serious enough."

Mo sits next to her nephew. "What's so fascinating?"

"What?"

"There must be something really interesting on that floor."

He drags his gaze up, meets her eyes briefly, and looks away.

"Tough way for the season to end, huh?"

"I guess."

"It had to end sometime, though."

"Yeah."

"'Nothing lasts, for good nor ill.' Your grandfather Quinn used to say that."

Aidan returns to staring at the floor. Mo touches his shoulder lightly and is surprised by how muscular it is. Steeling herself, she decides to test the most plausible explanation she's come up with for her nephew's silence.

"I guess you can tell the truth now, huh?" she says.

Without anything moving, darkness seems to slide over his face. Perhaps she imagines it, the creepiness of talking to her nephew in a jail cell warping her perceptions.

"What do you mean?"

"You know what I mean."

When he doesn't respond, she says, "Have you given any thought to what will happen if Rick Sherman doesn't come clean?"

He looks her full in the face now, and she reads desperation in his eyes.

"You did what you said you'd do, Aidan. You kept your word. Nobody will blame you for telling the truth now."

Mo hears a steady dripping, probably a leaky faucet in the

next cell. The ringing of the phone in the office in front seems to come from a long way away. When it continues to ring, Mo wonders where the jailer is. She imagines the two of them escaping, guns blazing, Butch Cassidy and the Sundance Aunt.

Then she remembers how that movie ended.

"How'd you know?" Aidan asks.

"I didn't. If I started with the premise that you were innocent, it seemed like the best explanation for what happened."

"Are you going to tell?"

"I've got nothing to tell. Just a theory. How did Rick get the coin?"

"He said he needed money to give to Rindeknect. I gave him what I had, which wasn't much, including the change in my pocket. I didn't miss the coin until later."

She has to fight the urge to wrap her arms around him. In his hard man-face she sees the little boy who called her his Auntie Mo-Mo.

"Do you think he did it? Killed that man? Those men?"

"I don't know, Aidan. I don't even know him. And even if I did, I guess you never know what someone is capable of doing until they do it."

"Could you tell the sheriff I'd like to talk to him?"

"You bet."

When Mo stands, he stands with her.

"Aunt Mo? Thanks. Thanks for believing I was innocent."

Now she does hug him, and after a moment, he wraps his strong arms around her. She feels him shake with the sobs he has been holding in for a long time, along with the truth.

Mo waits outside while Todd talks with Aidan. When Todd comes out, his expression gives nothing away.

"We'll drive him home in an hour or so," Todd says. "You want to take a little ride?"

"Where?"

"Out to the meth lab where we found the body. I can tell you about my conversation with Aidan on the way."

"Okay. But why?"

"I hear you're pretty good at noticing things at crime scenes."

"Are you sure it's okay?"

He leans back, hooking his thumbs in his belt loops, and grins. "'I'm the law in these here parts, little lady,'" he says, doing a passable John Wayne. "'And don't you forget it.'"

"Yes, sir."

"Car's back at the office. Let's roll."

"Lead on."

"Are you limping?" he asks as they walk back to the office.

"Fell off a bike when I was out looking for Mom."

"Hurt bad?"

"No. Just enough to give me a hitch in my get along."

He glances at her, grinning. "You can still talk Iowa farm girl."

"You know what the say. You can take the girl out of the farm . . ."

"You've come a long way from that farm."

They head out Church Road traveling south from town. He drives in silence, his eyes on the road, giving her a chance to steal a glance. His face is still handsome and youthful but shows signs of his worry and fatigue.

"Is it just you and Randy?" she asks. "You seem to be on call 24/7."

"I am. There are six of us here, actually, and I have deputies in three other towns. But we lost five deputies in the last round of budget cuts."

"I thought the state was fighting a war on drugs."

"They send down all sorts of mandated programs. They just don't send any money to fund them."

"That must make it tough."

He glances at her, his left hand resting on the steering wheel, his right elbow on the seat rest between them. "'It's a chancy job,'" he says in a voice she doesn't recognize, "'and it makes a man watchful—and a little lonely.'"

"Who's that?"

"'I'm that man. Matt Dillon, United States Marshal. The first man they look for, and the last they want to meet.'"

"No offense, but I've seen reruns of *Gunsmoke*, and you, sir, are no James Arness."

He laughs. "Actually, that's William Conrad. He was the radio Matt Dillon. I listen to the old tapes."

A voice crackles on the police scanner, and Todd leans forward, listening attentively. Mo can't understand what the voice is saying, but Todd apparently can. He leans back, eyes flicking from the road to her. "We manage," he says. "Things are usually pretty quiet around here. Until recently, anyway."

His glance lingers on her. "Aidan didn't do it," he says.

"What did he tell you?"

"The truth. Sherman was Rindeknect's drug runner for the football team. When things started to get hot, he persuaded Aidan to hold his stash. The reasoning was, if a player got caught holding, he'd get suspended, and the team could afford to lose a lineman a lot more than the star quarterback."

"Aidan took one for the team."

"Exactly. Sherman promised Aidan that, if anything happened, he'd come forth as soon as the team won the championship."

"Or got eliminated."

"I don't think the kid's old man would let him consider losing as an option."

"What about the murders?"

"Aidan says he doesn't know anything about them."

"And you believe him?"

"Yep."

"Why?"

"Sheriff's intuition."

"I didn't think you could use that anymore, in this age of DNA testing."

"They haven't completely replaced the human factor. At least not around here. Actually, I'm still hoping the lab turns up something, but that takes weeks."

"Any theory on who did it?"

"Sure. I've always got a theory."

"Care to share it?"

"You show me yours first." The grin again. Todd is still the quizzical, sometimes mocking boy she fell in love with in sixth grade.

"Who says I've got a theory?"

He looks at her, eyebrow raised, head tilted. The car hits a pothole, wrenching the steering wheel from his grip, and he directs his attention back to the road. "Oh, you've got a theory, all right," he says.

"Rick Sherman would have to be a prime suspect," she says.

"Yep. I'm going to swing by the hospital after I drop you off and see if he's up to having a little chat. He might have killed

Rindeknect, but I don't think he killed Grimsled. I think Rindeknect did that."

"More intuition?"

"Grimsled was killed up close and personal. One quick blow to the face. The killer knew just where to hit."

"He drove the nose cartilage up into the brain?"

Todd looks surprised. "How'd you come to know a grisly thing like that?"

"Self-defense training."

"I'd better watch my step around you. Anyway, whoever killed Grimsled probably had some training in martial arts."

"Rindeknect?"

"He knew enough to give some of the kids lessons."

"Was there anything this guy couldn't do?"

"Stay alive. Somebody caved his head in with a pipe. We figure it had to be somebody he knew pretty well. There was no sign of forced entry or struggle. Rindeknect must have let the guy in and, at some point, turned his back on him."

"And you think it was Rick Sherman."

"He's the best we've got right now. We're almost there."

Todd noses the car onto a long, winding dirt lane, lined with thick bushes and wide enough for only one car. Ahead, an old barn lists to the right; parts of the sagging roof look rotted through.

"They've aired the place out," Todd tells her as he slows for an erosion gully before easing the car to a stop beside the barn's open double doors. "But I still want you to wear a gas mask and gloves. And don't touch anything. We'll just take a quick look around."

He sets the emergency brake and turns to her. "You sure you're up for this?"

"Oh, yeah."

As she gets out of the car, not waiting for him to come around to open the door, she feels her heart pounding with excitement. She's never seen a meth lab, has no idea what to expect.

And this particular meth lab, she reminds herself, was also the scene of a brutal murder.

18

A uniformed deputy sits in a folding metal chair, leaning back against the barn wall, Mountie-style hat pulled low over his eyes. The barn's open double doors sag on their hinges. A dirt ramp, overgrown with weeds and scrub grass, slopes to the loft door on the right side of the barn.

"The Larsons owned this place when we were kids," Todd tells Mo as they approach. "They sold to a corporate farm 10, 12 years ago. The land's still being farmed, but there was no need for the barn and farmhouse. They'll just have to bulldoze it when we're done picking through it."

"What's that smell?"

"Anhydrous ammonia. Hey, Jimmy."

The deputy jumps up from the chair. "Sheriff," he says. "Ma'am."

"Monona, this eagle-eyed youth is Deputy Sheriff James Jantz Junior, the newest member of the force. Jimmy, this is an old, dear friend of mine, Monona Quinn."

"Ma'am," he says again, touching the brim of his hat. When he swallows, his protruding Adam's apple bounces.

"How long's it been, Jimmy? Three months?"

"Seventeen weeks, sir."

"Seventeen weeks! Well, hell's bells, young man. You're practically a veteran."

"Yes, sir," James Jantz Junior says, grinning.

"Everything copasetic here?"

"Sir?"

"Cool, calm, and collected?"

"Oh. Yes, sir. Downright boring."

"All part of the glamour of law enforcement, Jimmy. Ms. Quinn and I are going to take a little look-see inside."

"Yes, sir." He turns, bends over, pulls a couple of ugly canvas contraptions from a cardboard box next to the chair, and hands them to Todd.

"You ever wear one of these things?" Todd asks, handing Mo one.

"What is it? It looks like a huge insect's head."

"Old-fashioned gas mask. My dad had a couple of these, surplus from the war. Me and Gary Martin used to play army with them. You remember Gary? He was a year ahead of us, starting guard on the basketball team. Pull it on over your head and just breathe normally."

When she struggles trying to get the mask positioned properly, he helps her. The smell of the mask overwhelms even the chemical odor.

"Very becoming," he says, grinning.

He dons his own mask. Jimmy hands them each a pair of gloves long enough to cover Mo's arms to the elbows.

"We'll just walk through quickly," Todd says. His voice sounds as if he's speaking through a funnel. "Don't touch anything."

He pauses at the door to let her go in first. The dirt floor of the barn is strewn with trash and plastic tubing. A long bench holds coffee filters stained red, funnels, what looks to be rock salt, several lithium batteries, an open can of Drano, mason jars, and propane tanks. A flash of red catches her eye, a scrap of wood, its paint faded, white letters spelling out what looks like the right half of an "O," an "R," and most of an "M." She reaches out to touch it, feels Todd's hand on her wrist. He shakes his grasshopper head. Right. No touching.

She almost trips over a scuba tank.

Sunlight filters through gaps in the roof. She hears the alien rasp of her own breathing. The plastic eyeholes fog up, and she can barely see. They reach the end of the barn, turn, and walk up the other side, which contains a double sink, also stained red.

As soon as they get outside again, she tears off the mask and sucks in clean, cold air.

"People actually worked in there!"

"That they did. It's a wonder they didn't blow the place up."

"Was that blood in the sink?"

"Iodine."

"Where was . . .? Where did you find . . .?"

"The body? Halfway under the sink, with his head staved in. It looked like he crawled there from across the room."

"How awful!"

"People usually die a lot slower than in the movies."

"Could any of the chemicals in there hurt you?"

"Oh, yeah. You can get burned, poisoned. The anhydrous ammonia sucks the moisture out of your skin tissue. The vapors can cause blindness, damage your lungs, even suffocate you."

"I'm surprised all that junk is still in there."

"Maid's week off, I guess."

"But don't they bag it all for analysis?"

"You mean like on *CSI*?"

"You're going to tell me it isn't like on television."

"We picked up anything we thought might be helpful and sent it to the lab. It'll be weeks before we get anything back. That's law enforcement in the boondocks, kiddo."

He leads her to the back of the barn, where a car has worn ruts through the tall prairie grass. "Just like a gopher's den," he notes. "They made themselves an escape route."

He begins walking down the makeshift road, and she hurries to match his long, athletic strides, glad she's wearing sneakers.

"If you think making the stuff is dangerous—and it is—," he tells her as they walk, "ingesting the finished product is even worse. It basically fries your organs. Your teeth turn yellow, or gray, or black. Then they fall out. You scratch yourself bloody because it feels like there are bugs under your skin. You don't bother eating or sleeping. You get extremely paranoid. Oh, and you smell like mayonnaise. Or glue."

"Why would anyone take that stuff?"

"Supposed to be the best high there is, I guess. And highly addictive. Worse than crack or heroin, I'm told. A lot of people get hooked on their first hit."

"Why here?"

"In Summerfeld? The stuff's everywhere now. Actually, this is an ideal location for a set-up like this. The state highway gives the traffickers a good north-south corridor, and I-80 links east and west. Randy can tell you how much of this poison they seize through highway interdictions."

"Not that I mind the walk, but where are we going?"

"Not far. I just want to show you where they dumped the waste."

She soon sees. The riverbank looks as if there's been a fire.

"The river looks okay, though."

"It's what you don't see. No fish, no bugs, nothing. And notice you haven't heard any birds singing around here."

Something had been missing. That was it.

"Birds are smart," he says. "They clear out when dangerous animals invade their territory. There's a falls a little ways upriver. Would you like to see it? Something pretty to erase the mess you've just seen?"

"I'd like that."

He slips through the tree branches and grasses where Mo sees no opening.

She follows him, discovering a small footpath through the forest of birch, aspen, pine, and oak. Todd holds the branches so they don't snap back into her.

"Notice anything unusual in the barn?" he asks without turning his head.

"It was all unusual to me. But no, nothing I can think of that might be helpful."

"It was worth a shot. Listen, you can hear the falls."

They emerge onto a small rock ledge overlooking a waterfall perhaps eight feet high. Hissing water tumbles into a frothing pool below.

He sits and pats the rock next to him. "Room for two," he says.

Mo sits. She has a momentary spinning sensation as she looks down into the river and grasps Todd's arm tightly with both hands.

"You okay?"

"Yeah. Okay."

Todd scoops up a few small rocks, shakes them as if about to toss dice, picks one out and lofts it out into the river. It lands with a soft kerplunk halfway across.

"You've still got the arm," Mo says.

He laughs. "On my best day, I couldn't throw like that Sherman kid. I've never seen a high school kid throw the ball 60,

70 yards, on the run, and drop it right into the receiver's hands like that. He's something special. Or was."

Another rock arcs out, plunking a few feet farther across.

"You weren't bad."

"In my day," he finishes for her, grinning. "And how about you? We all figured you could do and be anything you wanted. You can't believe how proud Mr. Clement was when you got your column with the *Trib.*"

"I wrote to him once, told him what an inspiration he'd been. He wrote back, the nicest little note. He said if I insisted on giving him any credit for my success, he guessed he'd have to let me."

Todd fires another rock. This one splashes a few feet from the far shore. "It really shook me up," he says, "when you went off to the big city. I guess I figured we'd always…" He shrugs.

"You went away, too."

He laughs. "All the way to Fort Wayne, Indiana. The big time! I figured it was just the first step and that I'd wind up someplace like Chicago, working homicide."

"Why did you come back?"

"Sheriff Possun called and said he needed a deputy and wanted me. I was flattered. My folks were here, a lot of my friends, people I'd grown up with."

He fires another rock. It comes within inches of the far bank. "Turns out Sheriff Possun was grooming me to run for sheriff when he retired. I did. And won."

"You sound surprised."

"I was. It was as if the town called my bluff."

"I can't imagine anybody voting against you."

"Oh, there were a few." He smiles and turns his head to look out over the river. "Did you ever wonder?" he asks. "What might have been?"

"Sometimes."

"I was still on the rebound when I got married. My dad tried to warn me, God bless him. But who listens, huh? Daddy was right, of course. The marriage was pretty much a train wreck from the beginning."

She feels the force of his exertion. The rock hits the far bank but rolls back into the river. He turns to face her. "I told myself it was because you were going to be a nun."

"A nun!"

"You should be flattered." He reaches out to take her hands. "I guess I could handle the thought of losing you to God. I took some comfort in the fact that you didn't marry. I . . . That was pretty selfish. I told myself I just wanted you to be happy."

"Todd, I . . ."

"Wait. Just let me say this. No strings attached." He releases one of her hands. The backs of his fingertips brush her cheek. He takes a stray strand of hair, tucks it back behind her ear.

"I never stopped loving you, Monona. I tried to talk myself out of it a million times. I could convince my head, but my heart would never buy it."

He leans forward. She feels herself leaning to meet him. His soft, cool lips send a current through her, and warmth spreads from her groin into her stomach and chest. She feels herself melting into him.

She puts a palm on his chest and pushes gently; he immediately releases her.

"Mo, I . . ."

"It's alright."

"I didn't plan this, believe me. I . . ."

"It's as much my fault as . . ."

"I just wanted you to know . . ."

They both stop.

"You're married. I respect that. I wouldn't try to make you do anything to mess that up." He laughs. "Not that I could. You may not have become a nun, but you're the most religious person I've ever met."

"Religious?"

"I mean it in a good way. Not 'holier than thou.' Spiritual." He turns so that he's facing her. "But I can't believe you don't still have feelings for me."

She meets his eyes. Those amazing eyes. Two decades melt away. She's not sure who initiates the second kiss. She closes her eyes and feels herself falling; she waits for the water to rush up to meet her.

His hand is on her breast, her stomach. He should stop. He has to stop.

She has to make him stop—

"Todd!"

He removes his hand, shifts his weight away from her. She still feels his hand. They sit side by side, looking at the frothy water below. Has it been a minute? An hour? The sun is high overhead. Is it the same day? The same sun?

Once, early in their relationship, he'd taken her to a movie and to Bev's afterwards, and they'd talked for a long time. When he took her home, they stood on the porch, first talking, then kissing, and after what had seemed a few minutes, she opened her eyes to see that the predawn had begun to light the eastern sky.

"We'd better go back," she says.

"Yeah."

He jumps up nimbly and gives her a hand up. Their bodies brush together on the narrow ledge. He hops off and reaches up to help her. She lands awkwardly, her ankle twisting slightly.

"You okay?"

"Fine. Lead the way. My sense of direction stinks."

"You always gave me the impression you knew exactly where you were going."

He plunges into the thicket of brush. She follows, the branches scraping and poking her. The sound of rushing water floods her, as if someone just switched the falls back on.

The dream of the night before returns to her, and now she sees clearly the face of the man making love to her.

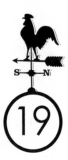

Danny spots the car first and charges down the driveway. Maddie watches from the porch as the car makes its way slowly up the drive and stops just short of the house.

"Mom! Mom!" Danny runs to the porch. "He's here! He's here!"

He turns and runs back to the car, where Aidan, Todd, and Mo are emerging. Danny takes his brother's hand and tugs at him to hurry, but Aidan walks slowly, head down. Danny drops Aidan's hand and runs up the steps, Mo following.

Todd and Aidan stand in shadow at the foot of the steps, Aidan with head down, hands clasped in front of him.

"Good heavenly days!" Grammy Quinn says from the doorway. "You just going to stand out there with your tongues hanging out? Get inside, right this minute!"

They troop into the living room. Grammy Quinn plops down in the rocker.

Aidan sits in the recliner, and his little brother wriggles up beside him. Mo and Maddie sit together on the couch. Todd takes the wing chair by the window.

"Isn't anybody gonna talk?" Danny asks.

"Would anyone like some tea?" Maddie asks at the same time.

"Oh, piddle," Grammy Quinn says, snorting. "I'll bet the sheriff would like a beer. Wouldn't you, young man? I think Aidan could probably use one, too. Heck, I think I'll have a beer!"

"Me, too!" Danny says.

"Thanks, but I'm on duty," Todd says. "Maybe I could just have whatever the young man's having." He smiles at Danny. "What's your drink, partner?"

"Root beer!" Danny says, beaming.

"Two root beers, coming right up," Maddie says.

"I don't want root beer!" Grammy Quinn insists. "I want beer beer. And I think Aidan deserves one, too, all they've put him through."

"Mother!" Maddie says.

"I quite agree," Todd says. "But root beer will be fine for me."

"I'll get them," Maddie says, starting to get up.

"You sit, Sis. I'll get them," Mo says.

"They're in the fridge in the basement. The tall glasses are in the cupboard on the service porch."

"We don't need glasses," Grammy Quinn says. "Just bring the bottles!"

Mo clicks on the light switch at the head of the basement steps. A bright light goes on overhead and then, a second later, a much dimmer light flickers on downstairs. Mo grips the handrail and takes the steps carefully. The air is cold and dank in the basement. The old furnace huffs in the corner, and Mo wonders if Maddie still waits until November first to fire it up each year, regardless of how cold the October nights become.

She finds the drinks and carries them between her fingers by the bottlenecks, three in each hand. The bottles are cold, and they begin to sweat when she gets upstairs. Maddie has put out coasters. Mo distributes the drinks.

"To the jailbird!" Grammy Quinn says. "Thank God we sprung him!"

"I'll drink to that," Danny says, grinning. He and Grammy Quinn seem to be the only ones enjoying the moment.

Grammy Quinn puts the bottle to her lips before realizing that the cap is still on.

"Where's the bottle opener? You didn't bring a bottle opener!"

"It's a twist-top, Mom," Mo says.

"I'll open it for you, Mother," Maddie says.

She reaches for the bottle, but her mother hunches over it. "I can do it!" she insists. "I'm not an invalid."

She emits soft grunts as she struggles. "Damn it!" she snaps. She sticks the end of the bottle in her mouth.

"I believe this is a job for the law." Todd jumps up and crosses the room with long strides. "Mrs. Quinn, would you allow me the honor of serving you?"

"Why, thank you, sir. I'm delighted to see that chivalry is not dead."

"Not in the presence of a true lady," Todd says.

He takes the bottle in his right hand and dispatches the top with his left. He hands her the beer and raises his root beer in toast. "To freedom," he says, his voice low and rich and without a hint of sarcasm. "And to justice."

He and Grammy Quinn clink glasses and raise their bottles to their lips.

When Todd is again seated in the wing chair, he takes a second sip of his drink and places the bottle carefully on the coaster on the low table next to him. "We went to the hospital on our way out here," he says, nodding toward Aidan. "Our Mr. Sherman fractured his right wrist, and he has a severe concussion. His vision is still blurred, and he's on something pretty strong for pain."

"Will he be able to play?" Danny asks. He perches on the footrest, hanging onto Aidan's leg.

"Concussions are serious stuff," Todd says. "He'd be very wise to give up football."

"But he won't," Aidan says.

"I suspect he won't," Todd agrees.

"Was he able to tell you anything about the crimes?" Maddie asks.

"He admits he was running pot for Blind Ryne and that he gave the stash to Aidan to hold. He also admits coming out here to keep Aidan quiet and shake him down for money, which is how the coin wound up at the crime scene. But he insists he didn't have anything to do with killing Grimsled or Rindeknect."

"Do you believe him?" Danny asks.

"Yeah. Actually, I do. I never liked him for either murder." Todd glances at Aidan. "He told Aidan he was sorry."

"He should be!" Grammy Quinn says. She belches and murmurs, "'Cuse me," putting the back of her hand to her mouth. She drains her beer, sets the empty bottle on the hardwood floor, and burps again.

"So, who did do it?" Danny asks Todd.

"Who do you think did it?"

"Gosh, I dunno. Somebody very bad. Not Aidan!"

"No. Not Aidan." Todd shifts his gaze to Mo. "Do you have a theory?" he asks.

"I wouldn't call it a theory, exactly."

"A hunch, then?"

"I was thinking, wouldn't the same motives Rick Sherman had for killing Rindeknect also apply to his father?"

Todd smiles. "It was law enforcement's loss when you went into journalism."

"You mean his *father* did it?" Danny asks.

"Whoa, whoa, whoa! We're talking theories here. Or hunches." Todd nods toward Mo. "But I do intend to question Russell Sherman after I leave here. Which," he says, putting his hands on his knees and bending forward to stand up, "better be right about now."

"Why don't you see him out?" Grammy Quinn says, and Mo realizes that her mother is talking to her.

"That's okay, Mrs. Quinn. I can find my way out."

"Nonsense. Monona, where are your manners?"

Reluctantly, Mo walks him out onto the porch.

"Mo, about earlier . . . ," he begins as soon as the door shuts behind him.

"It's okay. Really."

"No. It isn't okay. I feel bad about it."

"Don't. I'm not really a nun, you know."

"No, but you are . . ."

"Married? Yes. I remember, thank you."

"God, Mo. I'm just making this worse."

"Todd, stop it. You didn't force yourself on me. We kissed. It was as much me as you, okay? No apologies necessary."

"Maybe not, but I am sorry."

"That bad, huh?"

"You know what I mean! And I'm sorry about Aidan, too. He's had a rough time."

"No apology needed there, either. My nephew got himself tangled up in bad business with bad people, and you had every reason to suspect him of worse. Now go catch a killer."

"Right." But still he lingers, his eyes on her. "I can't help what I feel, Mo."

"No. Nobody can do that."

"Not even you?"

She looks away.

"See you at Mass tomorrow?" he asks.

"I don't remember you hanging out much at church."

"I hang out there a lot now."

She nods, managing a smile. "I'll be there."

"Good. Okay, then."

He turns and walks slowly to his car.

Inside, Danny sits in the wing chair, looking tiny and subdued. Maddie is kneading her apron. Grammy Quinn's head has fallen forward, and she snores softly. Mo takes a step toward Aidan, but he throws a hand up, as if fending her off, and she steps back. The sofa bumps the back of her knees, and she sits, barely missing her sister.

"I'm sorry! I know I screwed up bad!" Fighting for control, Aidan looks up, eyes blurred with tears. "I don't even like weed. I tried it once, and it made me throw up. How dumb is that?" Sobs shake him.

"Then why, honey?" Maddie asks.

"I don't know. No! That's not true. I *do* know." He rubs at his eyes with his fist. "I wanted to be one of them. I wanted them to like me."

"You have friends," his mother protests.

"I wanted better friends! Important friends!"

He puts his head in his hands and massages his scalp. Danny watches him, his eyes stricken with concern. The rocking chair lets out a screech, and Grammy Quinn crosses the room to stand, arms crossed, looking down at Aidan.

"Look, Sonny Jim," she says. "What you did was wrong. And stupid. Learn from your mistakes and move forward. You hear me?"

He nods and mumbles something.

"How's that?" Grammy Quinn says.

Aidan looks up, eyes red-rimmed and filled with pain. "You've got every right to hate me," he says.

"Twaddle, I love you. We all do. Stand up. Hop to."

He shoves to his feet. His grandmother stands on her tiptoes and wraps her bony arms around him.

"Now, who's going to make my supper?" she says when she breaks the embrace. "I'm starving!"

"I'll get right on it," Mo says, relieved to be set into motion again, and she and Maddie rush to the kitchen to prepare a fast stir-fry.

During one of the frequent lulls in the conversation at the dinner table, Danny catches his brother's eye and says, "'I knew there wasn't no jail could hold you!'"

"What kind of talk is that?" Grammy Quinn asks.

"He's imitating Jimmy Cagney," Mo says, laughing. "You know, the actor."

"I know who Jimmy Cagney is."

"Actually, he's imitating Todd, Sheriff Brabender, imitating Jimmy Cagney," Maddie says.

"Who's Jimmy Cragney?" Danny asks, and they laugh again.

Mo catches Aidan's eyes on her. "What?" she prompts.

"It's just really weird when you and Mom laugh at the same time."

"What's weird about it?"

"I can't tell where one voice leaves off and the other begins."

"What a day, huh?" Maddie says as she and Mo clear the dessert plates and carry them into the kitchen after dinner. "You wash, I'll dry?"

"Sure."

"Nope." Aidan's voice comes from behind them, and they turn to see him standing in the doorway. "You sit. I'll wash and dry."

"You don't have to do the dishes, honey," Maddie protests. "We're just so glad . . ."

He takes the plates from his mother and sets them in the sink. "Don't move," he says. He disappears into the dining room and returns lugging two chairs, which he sets in the middle of the kitchen, facing the sink.

"Your job is to supervise," he says, indicating the chairs. "I figure it'll take at least two of you." He turns the hot water on full blast in the sink and rolls up his sleeves.

"No use arguing with the man," Mo says.

"Wouldn't do a lick of good," Maddie agrees.

But after a few minutes of inactivity, Mo stands, liberates a dishtowel from the rack, and reaches for one of the plates in the drying rack. Aidan gently places a hand on each shoulder, turns her, and sits her back down.

"Sit! Stay!"

Aidan empties the sink and stacks the pots and frying pan in it before again filling it with hot water.

"When was the last time you called Doug?" Maddie asks under the pounding of the water.

"Right before dinner."

"Did he pick up?"

Mo shakes her head.

"Oh, honey." Maddie puts a hand on top of her sister's. Her

face sets with resolve, just as it did when they were kids and Maddie had taken all the teasing she was going to. "You need to go back home," she says, "and take care of things."

"I have no intention of—"

"It's all right. Aidan's in the clear, or almost, anyway, and Mom seems to have stabilized for now. You've got to get back to your own life."

"You're sure?"

"Yes, I'm sure."

"You'll tell me the moment you want me to come back?"

"Oh, honey. I want you here all the time. But yes, I'll call when we need you."

"I don't know. I . . ."

Maddie's grip tightens on Mo's hand. "Listen to me, Sis. I don't know how I would have gotten through this stretch without you. But I'm worried about you now. You and Doug. You need to get on home."

Mo nods, anxiety swirling up in her. "You're right," she says. "I do need to get home."

She finishes the thought silently: to see if I've got any marriage left to go home to.

20

The recorded bells in the old tower of the basilica are playing "The Church's One Foundation" as they walk out into the clear, cold morning.

"Good day for traveling," Maddie says. "Darn. I was hoping for a tornado warning."

"Don't even joke about a thing like that," Mo says.

"Did somebody tell a joke?" their mother asks, catching up after pausing to critique the pastor's sermon for him.

"I'll say goodbye here," Mo says, turning and taking her mother's hands in hers. "It won't get any easier if I wait."

"Do you really have to go?" Danny wails.

"I really do."

"I don't want you to."

"Danny! Hush now," Maddie tells her son. "Aunt Mo has a lot to do back home."

"Why don't you just live here?" Danny presses. "You used to."

Mo squats down to get on eye level with her nephew. "Give me some love, Danny boy," she says, spreading her arms, and Danny tumbles into her embrace.

"I love you, Aunt Mo," he whispers in her ear.

"I love you, too, Danny. With all my heart."

She stands and receives hugs from her mother and sister, then walks over to Aidan, who has been hanging back.

"When I was a kid and made a mistake," Mo says, "—and believe me, I made plenty of them—my father, your grampa Quinn, always used to tell me to 'straighten up and fly right.' It isn't original, and it isn't especially profound. But he said it with such love and such caring, I wanted nothing more in this world than to straighten up and fly right."

"I hear you," Aidan says.

They embrace.

"Thank you so much," he says.

"Make me proud of you."

"I will."

"I know you will."

Mo wipes at her tears as she steps back.

Todd has been waiting at the fringe of the family circle and now steps forward. "Would you like police protection to your car?" he asks, smiling.

"I guess a girl can't be too careful."

She turns back to her family. "Okay." She takes a deep breath. "Launch time."

Maddie hugs her again, fiercely.

"Just call," Mo whispers to her sister. "I'll be here."

"I know. God bless you for that."

Walking down Church Street toward the square, Mo is acutely aware of Todd Brabender walking at her side. She has to remind herself that "having your heart in your throat" is just a metaphor. Something has surely lodged in her windpipe, and she finds herself struggling to breathe normally. She knows she's going to cry, but she also knows she won't do it until she's safely in the car and back on the road.

"This probably isn't the time or place," Todd says softly, and her breath catches, "but it's the only time and place I've got."

"Todd—"

"Let me talk. Please."

They reach the courthouse lawn. Two squirrels skitter around the trunk of an oak tree, their claws chewing the tree bark with a staccato chattering. She stops and turns to face him. He takes her hands in his, and she realizes that, despite the November chill, his hands are sweating. His eyes probe hers. His brow furrows in concentration.

"This didn't go very well when I practiced at home this morning," he says.

"You don't have to say anything, Todd. Really."

"Maybe not." His hands squeeze hers tightly enough to pinch the fingers.

"You know how I feel about you. I just want you to know that I'm here. I won't pray for your marriage to go on the rocks. I know how painful that is, and I love you too much to ever want you to be in pain. But if something does happen . . ."

"Shhhh." She wriggles her right hand free and gently touches his cheek, which is hot under her fingertips. "I know," she says. "I know."

He leans forward, and she realizes that he means to kiss her and draws back. "Please," she says. "I'd have to go back to confession!" She tries to laugh, but the sound gets strangled in her throat.

"Okay."

He turns away quickly, but not before she sees that tears have welled up in his eyes. She watches him walk swiftly back up

Church Street, nodding to a couple of parishioners who have lingered only briefly for hospitality in the church basement and are now walking home.

Her car is parked in front of the *Pentagram* office and Bev's diner on the far side of the square. Instead of taking a straight line across the park, she walks along the southern side of the square, passing Jill's Quilts and the mighty Majestic, both Sunday-morning closed, as is The Cowboy Craig Marvel Museum on the corner.

The hardware store and toy museum seem lifeless, too, but the sign in the door says Open, and, on impulse, she goes inside for a last look around.

The tinkling of the bell over the door announces her entrance.

"Hello?" she calls out. "Anybody here?"

She walks slowly up one of the narrow aisles, the shelves looming on both sides of her. She knows the door to the museum will be locked, but she reaches out and tries the knob anyway.

"Help you with something?"

She starts, taking a breath to ride out the adrenaline surge. "You startled me!"

Clabe Profitt steps out from between two shelves. "Something I can do for you?"

"Yes. I . . . That toy tractor you showed me the other day?"

He waits, his eyes darting everywhere but her face.

"I have a little nephew . . . my husband's, actually. I guess that makes him my nephew-in-law? Anyway, he's got a birthday coming up, and I think that tractor might be just right for him." She's surprised at how easily the lie pours out.

Profitt's hands are thrust deep in his pockets, and his bony shoulders are hunched forward. His small head perches on his skinny neck. He looks like a buzzard, a buzzard in baggy over-alls large enough to accommodate two of him.

"What's this nephew's name?" he asks, his voice a raw scratch.

"His name? Timothy. Could I take another look at that tractor?"

"I suppose." He digs the keys out of his pocket. Something like a smile bothers his face. Just a small-town merchant, after all, with an Iowan's natural reserve.

He unlocks the door and pushes it open, reaches in, and flicks on the light. "Go ahead."

He steps back, and she enters.

"Was that the McCormick or the John Deere?"

"I'm not sure."

"Over here. You can look at both of 'em."

"Which one would you buy?"

"For my nephew? If I had a nephew."

"Yes. For your nephew."

He sniffs, pulls a soiled handkerchief from his back pocket, and blows his nose copiously. "Like I said before," he says when he's finished, "you really can't beat that John Deere pedal tractor with the front loader. Let you have it for a hundret and ten, but that's as low as I can go."

She stoops to examine the shiny, red metal, pushing on one of the pedals to make the tractor roll forward.

"How old's this nephew-in-law of yours? Tommy, was it?"

"Timothy. Oh, he's just about the right age for it, I think. Although they grow so fast. Maybe I'd be better off just getting him some of the smaller toys."

She walks over to the cluttered counter, picks up one of the wooden pieces of a model under construction, and runs her thumb over the lettering.

"That stuff ain't for sale." He takes the piece from her and sticks it into the breast pocket of his baggy overalls. "You want that tractor or don't you?"

"I'll have to think about it and come back."

"I thought you was leaving town."

"I'll be back."

"Can't promise it'll still be here."

"I understand."

"I'll sell it to somebody. If it ain't you, it'll be somebody else."

"Yes. Of course."

"Be a shame to disappoint little Tommy, now, wouldn't it?"

"Timmy," she says, taking a step back. "His name's Timothy."

Her mind is racing, preternaturally alert. This moment seems etched—the dust, the smell of confined space, the beauty and waste of all the unused toys, the cadaverous man in front of her, the baggy overalls with pieces of wood sticking from the pocket.

"If the money's the problem," he's saying, "you could put a little something down on it now, and I could hold it for you."

"Thank you. I really have to be going."

She has to fight the urge to run. She hears him behind her, his slippered feet shuffling on the wooden floor. She hurries up one of the narrow aisles, brushing against something that clatters to the floor behind her. Outside, she risks a glance back into the store but doesn't see Clabe Profitt.

She walks swiftly, glad she wore practical pumps, casual for church but comfortable for the long drive home.

Why in heaven's name had she lied about having a nephew? She really has no idea. Something drew her to that room, something she's supposed to see and understand, but whatever it is, it's eluding her.

She finds her car and heads east out of town, back toward the farm, with one more goodbye to make at the little family cemetery. No one is coming in the other direction, and she sees only a rusted, brown pickup in the rearview mirror. She drives as fast as she dares on the meandering country road. Still, the short drive seems to take an inordinately long time. Now that she's finally in motion, she feels a horrible urgency about getting home to Doug.

Her eyes flick to the rearview mirror; the beater pickup sways as it rounds the curve 20 yards behind her. She studies the road ahead, reading the landscape. Another half mile, no more, to the turnoff for Dunning-Quinn Road.

She checks the rearview. The pickup is sticking close despite her speed. She strains to make out the driver, even slowing a little to let the truck get closer. A man. She can't tell who it is.

She takes the left turn too fast. The car swerves into a skid, the loose rocks on the shoulder of the road pinging like bullets against the underside of the car. She steers into the skid, foot off both accelerator and brake, and when she regains traction, she straightens the wheel, the car lurching back onto the pavement.

She can see Maddie's pickup by the house. She longs to stop and hug them all again, but that would entail the agony of saying goodbye again, too. So she drives on, much slower now, and turns onto Cemetery Ridge Road.

The pickup appears in the rearview. Her car hits a bump, wrenching the wheel from her hands, and she instinctively hits the brake, sending the car into a slow skid. She rides it out, feeling foolish, and turns in at the entrance to the family cemetery.

She parks and walks slowly up the slope to her father's grave. When she is about halfway there, the pickup pulls in and creeps up the footpath between rows of tombstones. She missteps, turning her right ankle painfully, and almost falls. Her hip throbs from the bike accident.

And at last the pieces fall into place, and she knows. Before she turns and looks back, she knows she'll see the man who killed Blind Ryne Rindeknecht stalking her through the cemetery.

She has cornered herself.

She thinks of her cell phone, in her purse on the passenger seat of her car where she left it.

She hears nothing but her own labored breathing.

With nowhere left to go, she turns and faces the killer, her father's grave at her back.

21

"You should drive more carefully," Clabe Profitt says, walking slowly toward her.

She could scale the fence easily enough but doesn't dare turn her back on him. She forces herself to breathe deeply and slowly, gathering her strength inside, as her self-defense classes with Suzanne the Warrior Goddess have taught her. Her stalker is scrawny and looks ill suited for hand-to-hand combat. He's wearing slippers. You can handle him, she tells herself.

He pulls a hand gun from the hip pocket of his baggy overalls and levels it at her.

She raises her hands slowly, registers the gun, and drops them.

"You killed Blind Ryne."

"Yep."

"Why?"

"Because the doped-up fool was going to take everything I worked for all my life."

"You owed him money."

"My luck woulda turned, but he was leaning on me to pay him now."

"And my nephew provided you with a perfect cover."

Profitt grins, showing crooked, yellowing teeth. "Yep."

"Did you kill Grimsled, too?"

"Nope. I figure Ryne did that hisself."

He takes a step forward. He's now no more than six feet from her. Could she charge him before he fired the gun? Keep him talking, she tells herself. Use patter to divert his attention from the magic trick.

Only, she has no trick, no magic rings, no dancing handkerchief.

"You won't get away with this," she says, sounding like a bad movie.

"Sure I will. You ain't going to tell anybody."

"Who will you have to kill after you kill me?"

He shrugs. "Nobody, I hope. Whoever I need to, I guess." He laughs, wiping his nose with the back of the hand holding the gun. "You figure your boyfriend's gonna hunt me down, do you?" He makes another swipe at his nose. "I plan on dumping what's left of you where nobody'll ever find it. Nobody seen you in the store today, and nobody knows we're out here now. You're just going to disappear."

"He'll figure out you killed Rindeknect."

"Maybe." Profitt straightens his arm and points the gun directly at her head. "Maybe not. Either way, you won't be around to find out."

Something moves at the corner of her vision, and she fights the urge to look. Wrecker ambles up the road and turns in at the cemetery. Seeing her, he begins to trot, tail wagging, ears up.

"Stop!" Mo says sharply.

Wrecker's ears drop, and he sits, eyes on her.

"You going to start begging?" Profitt asks. "I think I'd enjoy that."

"I'll bet you would. Wrecker!"

The dog's head pops up.

"Attack!"

Profitt breaks into a jag-toothed grin and actually giggles. "You've been watching too many bad movies, girlie," he says, "if you think I'd fall for—"

With that, he goes down under the weight of 65 pounds of confused but willing mutt.

The gun flies from Profitt's hand and lands in the grass to Mo's right. She pounces on it.

Profitt struggles to his feet. She points the gun at him. Wrecker watches her, tail wagging, waiting for the game to continue.

"You didn't think I was really gonna shoot you, did you?" Profitt asks.

"Weren't you?"

"'Course not."

"You had me fooled."

"There you go! Big joke! Now why don't you just hand that thing over before somebody gets hurt?"

"Fool me once," she says, "shame on you."

"You couldn't shoot me."

"I'm pretty sure I could."

"You even know how to use that thing?"

She examines the gun in her hand. "It's loaded. The safety's off. All I have to do is pull the trigger. I know to aim for your upper torso. I know to empty the gun into you because one shot likely won't kill you."

The smile slides off his face. "Come on, now, girlie."

"Mr. Profitt, I'm about mad enough right now to shoot you just for calling me 'girlie.' Maybe you'd better just shut up for a bit."

"Yes, ma'am," he says.

He doesn't say another word as Mo walks him to her car, retrieves her cell, and calls 911.

Then they wait for Todd to come.

"Have you ever shot a gun?"

"Nope. Never have."

Maddie and Mo sit on Maddie's porch, both bundled in parkas, hoods up against the chill of a late afternoon breeze from the north. The sun is sinking behind the trees, already far to the south now, winter well on its way. Maddie sips her green tea, Mo her black coffee. Chance, Danny, and Grammy Quinn have taken Wrecker for a walk.

"Would you really have shot him?"

"If I had to."

Maddie shivers, pulling the parka tight around her throat. "I don't know how you do it. I would have been so afraid."

"You think I wasn't?"

"Were you?"

"Sis, I was terrified! I never want to go through something like that again." She hears herself telling Doug the same thing twice before, and her heart quickens with a mixture of dread and anticipation at the thought of seeing him.

"I'm just real glad you taught Wrecker to attack on command," she says.

"I didn't."

Mo looks at her sister. "Who did, then?"

"Nobody, as far as I know. He must have picked it up on the street, because he sure didn't learn it from anybody around here."

Now it's Mo's turn to shiver. "That's some dog," she notes.

"What made you suspect Clabe Profitt?"

"Something I'd seen at the murder site. A scrap of wood. It kept nagging at me, but I couldn't quite put it together."

"That's what prompted you to go to the museum today?"

"I guess so."

"And something in the museum told you he was the murderer?"

"He put a scrap of wood from one of his models into his pocket. At the cemetery, I finally remembered I'd seen a scrap like it at the crime scene. It had the letters 'ORM' on it. I didn't recognize that as being part of the 'McCORMICK' signature then, though."

"But he thought you knew, and that's why he followed you out to the cemetery."

"Yep."

"Where you disarmed him and took him into custody."

Mo laughs. "Where Wrecker and blind luck saved my hide, you mean. I was lucky."

"That's the third time you've had that kind of luck."

"All this good luck could get me killed."

Maddie takes a sip of her tea, holding the mug in both hands to bring it to her lips. "Luck had nothing to do with it," she concludes.

"Must have been my natural talent as a sleuth, then, huh?"

"Nope. Wasn't that, either. Do you want more coffee?"

"I'll go in with you. It's getting too cold out here for sitting.

"So, if it wasn't luck, and it wasn't all those Nancy Drew books I read as a kid, what was it?" she asks in the kitchen, getting her refill.

"I don't believe in coincidence, kiddo. I see the hand of God in this."

Mo nods thoughtfully. "I see the hand of God in every-thing," she says, "but only when I look back. At the time, it all seems like blind curves and dead ends."

"Why don't you stay one more night, Sis? There's no point in driving all that way tonight. Besides, it looks like it might be blowing a storm this way. And we're having meatloaf."

"Dad's favorite. That, and what he always called 'meat cakes.'"

"A plain hamburger patty, not even salted, served with mashed potatoes, no butter, and whatever vegetable was handy. The man liked his food simple."

"Couldn't have been much fun to cook for." A huge sigh escapes her. "I'd love to stay. You know I would. But I really need to get back."

"I understand."

"The funny thing is, when I leave here, I won't know whether I'm driving toward home or away from it."

"Both, maybe."

"We share a lot more than memories, kiddo," Mo says.

"You'll call me as soon as you get home?"

"I will."

"And we've got email down on the farm now, you know. There's no excuse for us not to stay in touch."

"Every day."

"Promise?"

"I promise."

Mo looks deeply into eyes the exact shape and blue-green color as her own. "God bless you," she says. "I love you."

The front door slams, and Wrecker's desperate claws clatter on the hardwood floor in the living room. The dog slides past the kitchen door, gathers himself, and gallops in, his entire hindquarters wagging.

"What's for dinner?" Danny asks, charging in behind the dog. "Can Chance eat here?"

"Meatloaf. And yes, if it's okay with his mother."

"Oh, boy, meatloaf! My favorite."

"I thought mac and cheese was your favorite."

"Unless we're having meatloaf."

Mo laughs.

"Please stay for dinner, Auntie Mo," Danny says, running over to throw his arms around her waist.

"You could leave right after dinner," says Maddie. "Otherwise, you'd just have to stop for something to eat on the way."

Mo smiles, nods, and Danny cheers.

But the nervous dread that has been building in her whenever she thinks about returning home wells up again, and she wonders how Doug will greet her return.

Or if he'll even be there to greet her at all.

EPILOGUE

It is nearly midnight when she pulls her little del Sol into the dirt lot behind the *Doings* building. When she turns off the engine, silence engulfs her. Her little town is sleeping, its shops and diner closed up tight along Main Street.

She gets out and stretches. Her back aches, her legs are stiff, and she nearly loses her balance. She feels like a sailor trying to find her land legs after months at sea.

It begins to snow. Tiny ice pellets sting her cheeks and hiss as they touch the hood of her car behind her.

She walks around to the front of the building, where fresh copies of the *Doings* sit in the honor box by the door. They have indeed produced the weekly miracle without her. There's an important lesson here, she thinks, a lesson in humility.

She takes a thin, crisp copy of the paper from the box and scans the headlines in the dim light of one of the town's two streetlights.

MITCHELL TOWN COUNCIL
VOTES TO REJECT HIGHWAY EXPANSION

Father O would have been pleased. She smiles at the thought

of the dear, gentle priest, who had fought against what he saw as the potential desecration, not just of the Catholic cemetery, but of the town itself.

The vote is probably a futile gesture, but still, the council showed some backbone. Better to do what you think is right and go down fighting.

She folds the paper under her arm and walks down Main Street toward the café that still carries the sign "Charlie's Mitchell Diner."

Each little town is different, she reflects, but each has much in common with every other little town. In Summerfeld, Bev's had been and remains the center of community life, and in Mitchell, her new home, Charlie's serves that function, even though Charlie is gone.

Maybe wanting to move from Chicago to Mitchell was a way to try to go home again to that other little town of her youth.

She walks past "The Hair Apparent," known locally as "Syl's Clip Shop," to Starlite Video, where a light shows from the office in the back of the store. She raps on the window, raps again, and the proprietor, Dan Weilman, appears in his office doorway. His suspenders are down, and his pants ride low under his belly.

"You working late, too?" he asks, opening the door and stepping back to let her in.

"No, I'm just getting in."

"That's right!" He snaps his fingers. "You've been down visiting your sister in Iowa." He says 'I-uh-way.' "You want coffee? I got fresh in back."

"No, thanks. I was wondering if it's too late to rent a video."

"Danny Weilman's ready to turn a buck any time, day or night. What would you like?"

"Do you still have *Murphy's Romance*?"

"You bet. I'll get it for you."

She stands with her back to the counter, looking out at the diner, silent and dark, across the street.

"Here we go!" He slaps the plastic container on the counter. "It's due back Tuesday."

"Thanks."

"Pay me later. The take's all counted. It would just mess up the bookkeeping if I took your money now."

Feeling inordinately grateful, she walks back to her car.

"Almost home," she tells herself as she slips in behind the wheel. "Almost home."

The snow isn't sticking to the road as she guides the little del Sol past the Catholic church, dark and silent on the hill above the cemetery, and accelerates as she heads out the country road. She has to fight the conflicting urges to speed up and to turn around. Telling herself how foolish she is for being so nervous doesn't help. Never does, she reflects.

She takes the final bend in the road. The porch light glitters off the snow. A light shows in Doug's office window, downstairs and to the left of the front door. His CR-V isn't in sight, but he would have parked it in the garage.

She turns in at the driveway and begins the long, slow climb up the hill.

an excerpt from

Obsessions

the fourth Monona Quinn Mystery

by Marshall Cook

due out from Bleak House Books

Fall 2008

PREDICTABLY, THE "CONTINENTAL BREAKFAST" in the hotel lobby is a total loss. Dried out-looking bagels in cellophane and teeny plastic tubs of butter (margarine having apparently been outlawed in "The Dairy State") and cream-cheese-like-substance, to be spread with little plastic knives. Six or seven of the saddest-looking bananas he has ever beheld, adrift in the bottom of a huge plastic bowl. A bleak dispenser of murky cranberry juice. Two industrial-sized coffee urns, one with the black handle for high-test, one with the red handle for why-bother.

For reading material, a stack of something called the "Northwoods Summer Recreation Guide," put out by the Shepherdstown Daily Dispatch. The damn thing doesn't even carry a crossword puzzle. The "books" on the shelves lining the fireplace turn out to be mostly old VHS tapes and DVDs of Disney movies and third-rate comedies. Two shelves hold battered boxes of jigsaw puzzles that positively scream "pieces missing." The single shelf of actual books offers bodice-rippers, historicals, the inevitable Reader's Digest Pureed Abominations, and, for his morning dose of humility, a battered paperback copy of one of his own thrillers.

He decides, God help him, to take a walk. Isn't that what one does when confronted with the great outdoors?

But he can endure a little deprivation. After all, the price is right. In enticing him to serve as "Featured Writer in Residence" for the 42nd Annual Writing without Walls Northwoods Writer's Retreat, Herman Chandler had instantly agreed to his ridiculous speaking fee. (He still has trouble believing, after all these years, that people pony up that kind of money simply to be in his presence). Not that he doesn't merit star-billing. He is, after all, the author of the Spirit Sorenson amateur sleuth mystery series, the Lowell Street police procedurals, and seven stand-alone thrillers, all of which have sold briskly.

As Featured Writer in Residence, he only has to conduct one mystery/thriller writing seminar, deliver a "noon day forum" on the writing life (which will be a thinly disguised pitch for his books), and give an evening reading/signing for the public. That leaves him plenty of time to prey on writer wannabes.

Chandler had also dangled the opportunity to share in a "truly unique and creatively invigorating community of writers in a beautiful natural setting." Well, not quite. Not by a damn sight, in fact. But the excursion did promise two weeks' diversion, something he desperately needs.

Truth is, he hasn't written anything in over three months. Every time he straps himself in at the computer and attempts to launch another Spirit Sorenson or Lowell Street, he feels physically ill. He's sick to bloody death of both of them; his only inspirations involve clever ways to kill them off.

He even tried starting a project starring both of them, a crossover, "Superman and Batman in one great comic book," as the World's Finest comics of his childhood had promised.

That made him doubly sick.

He supposes he's burned out, soul weary from staying in a succession of same Sheratons and Hiltons and having to get up each morning and put on Fletcher Downs, Author, and go make nice-nice with the book-buying masses.

Two weeks in the northwoods of Wisconsin, along with a hefty paycheck for very little work, sounded appealing.

He wanders down the dirt road, wading through thigh-high fog from the slough to the side of the road. He jams his hands deeply into the pockets of his windbreaker, wishing he'd brought something more substantial. How can it be so bloody cold in late July? Reeds and shrubs line the road, with forest starting perhaps 15 feet back on each side. The trees seem to be of all sorts: firs—or pines, he can never remember which is which—some sort of birch, and what he assumes are oaks.

He can't remember if he passed a convenience store on his way to and from the campus the day before. They seem to be everywhere now, and some of them even have decent coffee and the local newspaper, though God knew what that might be out in this wilderness.

The slough on his right twists off into the trees. He hears rustlings—birds? Squirrels? What other creatures do the woods contain? He hasn't thought to be afraid, and he dismisses the notion now. If the locals he's encountered can survive here, he certainly can, too.

He shivers. Why in hell doesn't he just go get the rental car and drive into town? But what if she's awake, and looking for him? He decides not to risk it and tries walking faster to warm up.

A noise to his left startles him, and he whirls to see a flash of white disappear into the trees. A deer? At least the hind end of one. He feels a flush of satisfaction.

The locals shoot them. He shudders at the thought. They probably mark their sons' faces with the blood.

Not a bad setting for a thriller, though his previous books have all had urban settings. Something elemental and dangerous about the woods. Maybe he'll cross genre and combine thriller, horror, and mystery. The locals have supplied him with a legendary creature, something they call the Humdrung— pure humbug, of course—a cross between a T-Rex and a Gila monster, with scales and tail and fangs and crossed eyes. They sell little stuffed Humdrungs in all the stores in town.

He rounds a bend in the road and discovers nothing more than the same nothing he has been walking through. He's cold in earnest now, and the prospects of finding a clean, well-lighted place seem dim.

He turns and retraces his steps, crossing over to the other side of the road. A pickup truck rumbles toward him, slowing and swinging to the far side of the road to give him a wide berth. The driver surprises him by waving, and Fletcher belatedly waves back.

They could at least have some sort of mom and pop 'general store,' he thinks bitterly. Everything seems to be 'mom and pop' here. "Fuzz and Doris' Bide-a-Wee Lodge." "Red and Ruthie's Humbug Supper Club." "Pete and Brenda's Do-Drop-Inn."

He snorts, remembering a sign he spotted in town advertising "GUN'S, AMMO, AND PHARMACY." What a combination. At least the owner spelled "pharmacy" right.

He passes the billboard announcing his "resort" a quarter of a mile up on the right, with "RIDING STABLE'S AND CAMPGROUND'S" another mile past that.

Local folk are mighty liberal with their apostrophes.

Another noise from off to his left startles him. He stops to put a hand to his chest, bends over and takes several deep breaths, the cold air stinging his nostrils.

Just another deer, he tells himself. Nothing to be afraid of.

He hears another noise—not a deer, a footfall on the road. He starts to straighten up and turn. Searing pain rips through his skull for only an instant before everything goes black.